# THE KEVINA PAUL SERIES:

# The Enigma

## M VYAS

Sept 2/25
Nov 5/25

PUBLISHED BY EMSA PUBLISHING
http://emsapublishing.com

*The Enigma of Her Longevity* is printed in Century Schoolbook. Title font is Modeshcrift by Peter Wiegel. Subtitles in AR Julian.

Cover by Elise Abram
Credits: "Woman Standing on the Rocks watching Sea, Sunset, Dramatic" vitomirov/Depositphotos.com. "Future Spaceship. 3D Image. MY OWN DESIGN" Alexmit/Depositphotos.com.

# DEDICATION

Maya and Asha The future belongs to you.

# IN APPRECIATION

I deeply appreciate the efforts of my son Neel, my sister Usha and my friend Lyle for reviewing earlier versions of my manuscript. I thank my friends Pravin, Madhu, Andrew, Larry and my niece Raemi for their encouragement.

Finally, I am very grateful to Nisha, without whose support, I would not have completed this project.

# 1

It was a hot, blistering day. The outside temperature was somewhere near fifty degrees Celsius in the shade, and I wasn't anywhere near some shade. It felt like I was in an oven. Actually, it was much worse. I was perched precariously on a camel—terribly uncomfortable, sweating profusely, my lungs choked with the dust kicked up by the galloping animal. To top it off, I had just discovered the ground was much farther away on camelback than horseback—*frighteningly* farther away—rendering my previous and somewhat limited experience with horseback riding of little use. My pleas to the keeper who was jogging along with me to slow the animal's galloping pace had gone unheeded. He was well bundled up, shawl wrapped tightly around his face, covering his ears, nose, and mouth. Of course, I was not as well prepared. He could not hear me yelling, and obviously, did not expect to. In his long experience, a camel ride was just a unique thrill for tourists. He definitely knew there were no such opportunities in Europe and North America.

I wondered how many tourists actually enjoyed this activity. I wished I had declined all invitations for the ride. Of course, one had to pay for it, and what's more, at the end of the trip, a sizeable tip needed to be added to the agreed-upon payment unless you were impervious to nasty looks and mutterings in Arabic.

A bit earlier, when I had both my feet planted on terra firma—a much more agreeable situation for me—I had been given an in-depth explanation on the Pyramids. During the informative tour, the guide parroted facts about when they had been built, who had built them, how they had been built, and how much material had been used, as she had done repeatedly in the past. Later, in the theatre, I also watched with fascination at how the bodies of the ancient royal families had been mummified. I knew from my own research prior to my trip that with respect to the pyramids, while a lot is known, there is also a lot that is unknown which remains buried in the rubble of ancient history alongside the mummies.

Atop the camel, through the dust, I could see the pyramids in the distance—already about four thousand years old—and I wondered how long they would last against the onslaught of corrosive pollution being spewed out into the atmosphere in ever-increasing quantities. Over the centuries, Egyptians had done next to nothing to protect the pyramids. I was reminded of the observations of author Paul Theroux in his book, *Dark Star Safari*, written at the beginning of this century on his travels through Africa in which he comments on the Egyptians' lack of appreciation over the millennia, of their unique gift from its ancient history. According to Theroux, it was not until the early nineteenth century, when the ancient Rosetta Stone was deciphered by Frenchman

Jean-François Champollion, that the rage for Egypt and its travellers were launched. The Rosetta Stone is a granodiorite stele inscribed during the reign of King Ptolemy V in 196 BCE. Earlier travellers included predators, as well, but in time, modern tourism grew over the centuries to become an important industry in Egypt, providing jobs and advancement for many Egyptians. But at that very moment, my mind and my entire being were occupied by two and only two thoughts: how do I survive the ride, and when will it end?

I more than relieved when it finally ended. I thanked the camel owner profusely and tipped him handsomely—too handsomely, in fact, as if I were rewarding him for having saved me from some near-death experience. I made a solemn vow there and then to never go near the animal again and to discourage any and all of my kith and kin who would care to listen; I'm afraid, there are not many who would do likewise.

I started to walk over to the taxi stand when I heard my palmtop buzzing with an urgent message from my dad. I pulled it out of my pocket, and even in the dust, I could read: "This morning, Aunt Kevy passed away in her sleep. Funeral service will be held in a couple of days. Hope you make it back home in time. Dad."

I thought I felt the ground underneath me move after reading the content of the short, abrupt message with the unexpected news. I was in Egypt on her say-so. How could this have happened so suddenly? I steadied myself for a few seconds while I reread the text.

With haste, I hopped into the waiting taxi—I'd hired it earlier from my hotel for my trip to Giza—and immediately called my dad on the palmtop to tell him I'd just received the upsetting e-mail.

"Yes, we've been trying to call you for a while. Where are you, anyway?"

I answered his question simply, which is what I normally do when my dad asks me a question. "I was on a camel."

"Riding a camel? That's dangerous!" Dad's voice, laced with concern, and not without a bit of impatience, continued, "Look, get off the camel. Aunt Kevy is no more. I heard about this about a couple of hours ago. I'm trying to get more details, but you must get back here by the next flight. I'm sure she'd want you to attend her funeral, which I understand will be in just a couple of days. If I hear anything more, I will let you know. Get here ASAP."

It was a typical, to-the-point conversation with my dad, with no small talk. The way he'd said, "she'd want you to attend," with a finality in his tone indicated it had been the end of the discussion.

He was quite right—I simply had to get back to Toronto to attend Aunt Kevy's funeral, no doubt in my mind.

Aunt Kevy wasn't really my aunt, as she was neither my dad's aunt nor even my grandfather's. In fact, there wasn't a single person alive in the world who was her nephew, niece, son, or daughter. She was more of the entire world's aunt. At 137, Aunt Kevy was the world's oldest person. No one in recorded history had ever lived as long. Now she was no more, and that was quite saddening, for me in particular.

First, no one could remember ever seeing her sick. She lived alone in a comfortable retirement condominium and took frequent brisk walks in the mornings and evenings, usually accompanied by a young health care volunteer. She enjoyed honorary memberships at local tennis and fitness clubs, local theatres, and several social clubs. Restaurants in town would not charge her for her meals. She was invited as a guest speaker and lately, as an honorary guest at many local, national, and even international events in the city. She was still mentally alert and aware of important events around her, be they local, national, and even international, and she held strong opinions about them, which she frequently expressed on radio and TV. People in Canada enjoyed her presence and her talks, making her easily one of the most popular personalities in the country. Internationally, she enjoyed a popularity that was the envy of politicians the world over, though lately, on the advice of her doctors, she had to drastically curtail her travels.

Years rolled into decades; Aunt Kevy seemed frozen in time while the people around her came and went. She'd seen newborn babies come to this world, wither away into old age, and finally depart, while she remained like a rock in the middle of a river, watching the unending flow of time around her, always there and unaffected. Now that I'd seen the pyramids and mummified bodies, I could say that she was, indeed, a living, thinking mummy.

Her full name was Dr. Kevina Paul. Among her many accomplishments was a doctorate from the University of Ontario Institute of Technology in aeronautical engineering. In her time, she had been a globally recognized authority on aviation. After her 136th birthday, I was asked to run her biography in a twelve-part serial—which I'd largely completed, and Kevina had, in fact, reviewed—for the magazine for which I worked.

Months before my departure for Cairo, I'd shown her my library of visuals, pictures of her, captured at various stages of her life, including photographs over a century old, and a set of videos. She was thrilled, saying she appreciated the amount of time I'd spent in compiling the library. We spent several weeks going over it. Anecdote after anecdote poured out of her mouth as the memories flooded in while I either audio recorded her or frantically typed transcripts on my tablet.

Slowly, after several months' work, her entire life had, at last, unfolded before me: a stellar career in aviation, encounters with cyber-terrorism in a faraway country where she'd exposed a coup, and, significantly, her discovery of the secret to a long and healthy life, leading her to become the world's oldest person—ever. Remarkably, she'd shattered previous longevity records, not simply by days, months, or even years, but by decades. Over the past few decades, the Canadian health industry had spent considerable resources to research Kevina's achievements in health and longevity. Thankfully, people generally respected her privacy, rather than crowd her with curiosity and inquiries. Her health care nurses, condominium security personnel, and even the local police were quite mindful of her need for privacy during her ever-increasing popularity, and they worked diligently, and quite successfully, to keep the unwanted away and guard her privacy.

While discussing her adventure in cyber-warfare with me, she explained the cyber-terrorism plot she'd helped to identify and neutralize. She elaborated as to how an associated coup had been successfully thwarted. Listening to her, I was fully aware she was far more knowledgeable than I was or could hope to be, but she had a way of simplifying the technical aspects. In the end, I understood everything enough to narrate it for my magazine. This is important now that several decades have gone by and the governments involved have finally lifted the cone of silence that had been imposed on it, allowing me to reveal it in sufficient detail.

During our last review meeting, she'd said, "Look, you've put a lot of effort into your project on me, which I greatly appreciate, but why don't you take a break? Go far away. Don't even think about me. Relax, hit the reset button, and come back fresh. It'll also give the editors and reviewers at your magazine time to tidy everything up for your final review."

It was a great idea. It was also true that after months of research, multiple sessions, and writing and rewriting, I realized I'd totally immersed myself in her life. Kevina had dominated my landscape for so long, I'd begun to live and breathe her. At the office, my boss knew my need to focus fully on writing her biography and had directed all other assignments to my colleagues.

I'd completed a major portion of the manuscript for the serial. The next day at the office, I talked to my editor and mentioned the break to him and he immediately agreed.

"Okay, I think it's actually not a bad idea," he'd said. "Look, why don't you stop where you are and submit for an editorial review? Let them look at it, tidy it up, and get it ready for commencing publication since it's a serial. The editors will need about three weeks to clean it up, and then, when you're back, you can finish it off. That way, we'll all be up to speed, and we might have some comments for you to consider as well. Go ahead and come back refreshed. How much time do you need? How does two weeks sound?"

I agreed.

"Why don't you visit a historic place, like Egypt?" Kevina had urged when I mentioned that my editor had approved my request for a two-week vacation. She remembered I was a history buff and had always been interested in Egypt, where one of the oldest civilizations had existed some five thousand years ago. She went on to tell me all there was to know about the pyramids—their physical dimensions, their history, the controversies associated with them. She recommended I stay—or at least, have a meal—at the nearby, luxurious Mena House Hotel. She had told me that it had been established by an English couple sometime in the late nineteenth century and that the famous, English author, Sir Arthur Conan Doyle, and his wife had been one of the early hotel guests, spending quite a few months there. Several world leaders had also been guests at the hotel, Prime Minister Churchill, General Chiang Kai-shek, presidents Roosevelt and Carter, Prime Minister Begin, and President Sadat among them. Sadat was later assassinated, and I couldn't help but wonder if it hadn't been because of his meeting with Begin at the hotel. It was in the early 1970s that the Indian hotel management company, Oberoi, had taken over the hotel. Under their management, the hotel was transformed into one of the top hotels in the world.

Impressed, I remarked, "Amazing, Miss

Kevina. You're a walking encyclopedia. What a memory!"

"Well, I remember trivia very well, though at times I find it hard to remember day-to-day events. For example, right now, I can't even tell you what I had for dinner last night." She smiled.

"Neither can I," I said, somewhat consolingly and truthfully.

She burst into laughter, and I joined in. I believe her self-deprecating sense of humor and frequent laughter was another factor that contributed to her longevity and enduring health. It was infectious, and most people couldn't help but be affected by it. I have little doubt that sharing laughter with her helped my well-being, too.

Per her recommendation, I began to plan my trip to Egypt. After decades of political upheaval—the result of a technology-enabled revolution—I remember reading about the Arab Spring and its bloody aftermath which affected several nations in the region. The Arab Spring had lasted a nearly a decade, however, the Egyptians had recently ushered in democracy over several elections with huge voter turnouts. A climate of safety and security prevailed over Egypt, and there were positive reports in the international media on the progress the country had made. Democracy had gained a foothold in several Middle Eastern countries. Business—and the tourist industry in particular—was booming in the region. Most of the Arab countries had recognized Israel's right to exist and trade with Israel was growing. Egypt had gone through many upheavals in its history, but the pyramids were always there.

Walking around the pyramids earlier, I felt

15

as though she were there with me. She had been, in one form or another, by my side in a constant, unending conversation. I'd developed an intuitive feel for her psyche and thoughts on most issues, yet the e-mail from my dad was harshly real: Kevina was no more.

I was deeply saddened, but understood her passing, because I—like many others who had known her—wondered how long she'd be able to carry on defying the ultimate and the inevitable end. I thought about the inevitability of death and the indisputability of what the ancient Greek poet, Claudian, had said about death over two thousand years ago: "*Omnia mors aequat*" (Death makes all equal). I had noticed her slowing down, both mentally and physically, though she was still amazingly agile for her age. I felt that, for me, she had not passed away. I knew that, in some ways, our conversations would continue; in my mind, I would continue to hear her voice debating on many issues, including national and international events and technology and science. I had to cut my Egyptian vacation immediately short and be on my way to attend her funeral to say my final goodbyes.

I logged into the airline's website on my palmtop and paid a premium to book myself onto the earliest available flight out the next morning. The taxi continued to speed along the streets while rays from the setting sun seemed to illuminate every particle of dust in the heat. The streets of Giza seemed hotter, dustier, and more crowded than ever before—or was this simply my mind benumbed by the shock? I would dearly miss discussing matters on nearly any subject with her. I was on my way to say a final goodbye to her at her funeral, taking solace that, in writing about her, I would, in a sense, immortalize her.

Under a cool shower in my hotel room, I watched as the dust of the pyramids washed away from my body and disappeared, sluggishly, down the drain. An eagerness to get back to Toronto overcame me. I had an early morning departure, but I knew that I probably wouldn't be able to sleep until it was about time to get up.

I was not particularly hungry after my shower, even though I hadn't eaten for several hours, but I walked down to the Egyptian restaurant and settled for a meal and a change of scenery.

Back in my room, in bed, I thought of Kevina and remembered her advice to meditate each night before sleep. Though I'd listened to her patiently at the time, I hadn't really practiced it with any regularity. Now, after her death, I tried meditating in the manner she had prescribed with mindfulness, focusing on calmness and serenity.

Somewhere in the night, I must have surrendered to a deep and sound sleep, because I was awakened by the telephone announcing, "Good morning, sir. This is your wake-up call. The time now is five-thirty in the morning. The temperature outside is..."

It was not until I was on the aircraft and flying nonstop from Cairo to Toronto that the full reality of her death settled over me. In her death, she was already at peace, and I knew deep down that she was a person who had planned every day of her life. This was a woman who, it had seemed, worked according to some sort of life-script, which she'd most likely written herself. She knew exactly what she was doing or going to do in life. It seemed she had an uncanny awareness of the future before her, like an inner telescope into the future. This was a woman who was always in full control of herself, to the point where I figured she'd likely known and planned the exact moment of her death.

"So can you really foretell the future?" I'd asked once, wondering whether I'd learn that she had psychic powers.

She'd laughed. "Come on, no one can do that. I certainly can't, and I've never met anyone who can."

She'd dismissed any suggestion about anything magical even remotely associated with her, immediately and conclusively.

I was persistent and continued to dig into her past. "Tell me, Auntie Kevy, in terms I can understand: what's the one factor that's contributed to your longevity and the good health you enjoy?"

Her response had been short and simple: "I willed it to myself. I truly wanted to be this way, and I worked for it the best way I knew how. Of course, I had a bit of help from upstairs." She laughed.

I didn't quite buy that line and resolved to dig even deeper. "Come on," I said, "there must be something more to it. No one wants to die." I tried to inject some substance to prop up my argument and lessen my frustration by referring to my grandfather's death in his ninetieth year.

She held her line with a firmness and clarity that only she was capable of. "Yes, you simply have to will it. Most human beings give up on themselves too soon. They fall into the trap of blaming almost anyone for their failures except themselves, but I wouldn't succumb to the blame game. I harnessed the power of my mind and body, with some help from medical technology, and good luck, of course. More importantly, I willed it, and then I worked at it. You see, it's all about retarding the forces of senescence. I truly believe that one shapes one's own destiny, that the past, present, and future are all connected, and that your past and present determine where you'll be in the future."

"I get the feeling you subscribe to Sartre's existentialism, that you, as an individual, focus on yourself, shaping your own destiny, but I still don't believe it's that simple. There has to be much, much more than a gross simplification." I simply had to drill down to the core of her secret.

I mentioned Jean-Paul Sartre, the French existentialist and Nobel laureate, to get her to open up more with respect to the impact Sartre's thinking had on her. I knew she'd read his books and was generally sympathetic to his views. Sartre's main argument was that unlike objects, which are designed specifically to have a defined purpose—or, as he called it, an essence—humans arrive on earth without a specific objective, except—as is the case with all life—to simply exist. Where humans are different from the rest of the beings, however, is that they are endowed with the mental faculties to define their own purposes and move forward. The sheer logic of Sartre's basic argument that each sane human is fully responsible for his or her own actions impressed me. I continued a bit doggedly ahead and paraphrased Sartre to her: man first exists and later defines himself.

I summed up, "Sartre thought of humans as

'arbiters of our own essence.' Existentialism is about how to live one's own life and taking complete ownership of all our actions."

She replied, "So am I a Sartre-style existentialist? As we've discussed before, I think so too. One defines one's own destiny first through thoughts and beliefs and then by actions. The gift of human life is one without an objective, so an individual has to define it and then live to attain it. Think of this: on earth, we are the only beings free and able to study options, make choices, and then act. I decide what I am going to do, and I do it, but I want to take a more holistic approach, rather than going through it piecemeal.

"One cannot stop aging, which is simply the unending flow of time. My personal battle in life is against the senescence brought upon us with the advancement of age. I did not want to become a victim of the Tithonus error, where old age is extended but without the extension of youthfulness, which is much more important. You remember, don't you, the Tennyson poem written in the 1830s on how Tithonus asked for immortal life from God but not immortal youth?"

Actually, I didn't.

She reminded me about what Tennyson had written:

*I asked thee, "Give me immortality"...*
*But thy strong Hours indignant worked their wills,*
*And beat me down and marred and wasted*
*me, And though they could not end me...*
*Let me go: take back thy gift.*

"Amazing that you can recite that from memory," I said. Later, I verified it was a near-perfect recollection of the poem. I'd heard her give a similar lecture as a special guest lecturer at a recent Innovations in Medicine Conference. The only reason I went to the conference was because she was going to speak at the dinner. She had given me this lecture repeatedly.

Later, in the aircraft somewhere over the Atlantic, I saw a short e-mail update from my dad that said that it had been determined that Aunt Kevy had passed away peacefully in her sleep and that the funeral had been scheduled for three days from then.

Only after I unearthed the incredible events that had shaped her remarkable life did I begin to come to grips with the real answer to my question, and I wanted to tell her so. The sadness was that I never got around to telling her that I might've finally stumbled upon some understanding as to why she had remained alive for so long.

When I'd shown her pictures of her, Nigel, and Shelly, she couldn't contain the tears rolling down her cheeks, and I had to give her a few moments to compose herself. I once asked her what had been the hardest challenge in her long life, thinking she'd say it was her quest for good health or her deciphering the cyber-attack. I was surprised when she said, "Separating from my husband, Nigel, was the hardest challenge. It nearly broke me."

# 2

With his eyes only half-open, Nigel looked out the window, his wakeful state and the current wave of sleep continuing their seesaw battle. The countryside danced by his window to the clickety-clack grind of the turbo train's wheels. Outside his window, the sinking sun bade a reluctant goodbye to the long summer's day.

Nigel felt a general sense of contentment, having enjoyed a light meal with a glass of his favorite wine. This momentary state easily extended to his life in general. He had less than two years until what would be a fairly comfortable retirement with a healthy pension. He could retire now, though with a slightly reduced pension from his position as the company's director of financial services. Nigel had risen to the pinnacle of his career, and now, drained of ambition, he was content to coast along the remainder of his corporate life, and fade into blissful oblivion. He arrived at this juncture in his life quite uneventfully.

To his credit, he'd cultivated some well-qualified and smart young people he could rely on and put them in the right positions. He was a good judge of people, and this simple formula had worked for him. He'd operated within the confines of his little kingdom, seldom venturing beyond. His was a world of tranquility. It was as if he'd staked out a world of comfort just for him, his cozy little island in the river of time. Lately, his life could be summarized in a single word: comfortable, and that was just the way he liked it

As his thoughts ran down his mind's track, the turbo train—also referred to as the TT, or bullet train—surged ahead at an average speed over 250 kilometers per hour. Throughout much of Canada and the United States, the turbine-powered trains had resulted in the revival of rail transportation. Interestingly, the TT had contributed to solving the gridlock in the air by introducing a land-based, alternative mode of superfast transportation. Before the advent of the TT, air traffic had increased to supersaturation levels in North America. Infusion of technology in air traffic management and the construction of additional runways hadn't been enough to keep up with the meteoric increase in air traffic. The TT had become a great success. It was as safe as air travel—certainly cheaper—and to Nigel's delight, it was very comfortable and speedy.

In the seat next to him was his wife, Kevina. They'd coexisted in a mostly unexciting and seemingly normal matrimonial relationship for about three decades, and the early fires of their youth had been dampened by the tide of advancing age, mostly Nigel's. They'd settled into a state of resigned acceptance; they had each other's company.

Some time earlier, their daughter, Shelly, had been ill with incurable cancer, and as life trickled out of her, they both clung to her. With her death, the last and fragile crystals of the emotional linkage between Kevina and Nigel withered away to an emptiness. Nigel secretly envied Kevina's continuing vitality as his own had deserted him. She seemed upbeat, exercised regularly, and was a careful eater. He himself was in general good health, but she was in a great physical state and would be considered beautiful by any standard. When she went to the nearby gym to exercise for a couple of hours, he'd read or watch TV, wishing he had her energy for regular, vigorous exercise. He also knew that she had a sharp intellect, and for that, she was well respected, not only in her professional circles, but in their social group as well.

The meandering of his half-asleep mind was interrupted by Kevina tugging at his sleeve, saying, "Nigel, I'm going to walk up to the dining car. Do you need a hot chocolate or milk from there?"

He waved a no with his hand and a grunt of husbandly irritation. Kevina rose up from her seat and settled back into his previous state of semi-wakefulness. As the darkness of the night outside deepened, his consciousness finally lost the battle, and he succumbed to sleep. Sometime in the night, he was vaguely aware that the train had briefly stopped at a station or two.

He grew uneasy when the seat next to him remained vacant for too long a time; Kevina had not returned. Several hours later, he awoke, his anxiety heightened. He pressed the call button, and the attendant arrived a couple of minutes later.

"Yes, sir, can I help you? Would you like the menu?"

"No, my wife has been away and hasn't returned to her seat. Can you make an announcement on the PA asking her to come back? She may be in the restaurant talking to someone."
"Certainly, sir."

The attendant hurried away, only to return a few minutes later. Before he could say anything, Nigel asked, "Did you make the announcement? I didn't hear it."

"No, actually, I didn't need to. I checked the passenger list, and the seat next to you is vacant. I mean, it's unassigned." He showed him the passenger list.

"Unassigned? That doesn't make sense. You must've made an error." His agitation growing, Nigel continued, "Make the announcement. Fix your records. We're travelling together to Edmonton. Make sure you have the right names: Paul. Mr. N. Paul and Mrs. K. Paul. Toronto to Edmonton."

He dismissed the attendant with an uncharacteristic wave of his hand bordering on rudeness. Nigel rationalized his behavior and mumbled as if to convince himself, "Some computer glitch, no doubt."

Confused, Nigel dialed Kevy on his cell phone, but there was no response. He knew she'd always kept her phone close to her. He resolved to redial her in a few minutes.

He rose to conduct his own search. He proceeded to the dining car, ears primed to hear the announcement, but the dining car was deserted.

The waiter greeted him warmly. "Morning, sir. I just finished brewing a fresh pot of coffee. Would you like some?"

On hearing the word, coffee, Nigel automatically said, "Yes, thanks." He grabbed the cup of coffee but declined the offer of a hot breakfast, too disturbed to think of food. The train continued rumbling on, the daylight barely visible over the distant horizon. Nigel sipped the coffee and felt a deep burn in his empty belly. Now he was upset with Kevina and the attendant, too. He downed the coffee, walked briskly toward his seat, and confronted the attendant.

"Well?" he demanded. "Did you find your error? I still haven't heard the announcement."

"Sir, I've double-checked and even reconfirmed with our head office in Toronto that there were two seats booked for Mr. and Mrs. Paul from Toronto. Mr. Paul in seat 7E is for Edmonton, and Mrs. Paul in seat 7D was only to Thunder Bay. Our record confirms she left the train at that point. There's no point in making an announcement as she was seen leaving the train. I'm sure she's not on board. I'm afraid there is no error at all, sir."

Nigel dialed Kevy on his cell again and again, but there was no response, which was definitely unusual. Nigel suddenly felt heat on his face, his knees weakened, and his tummy was set ablaze. Beads of perspiration formed on his forehead. He tried to fight the panic and calm his mind so he could think clearly. His castle of comfort had begun to crash around him, a sensation Nigel hadn't experienced in a long, long while.

He continued to wallow in his sea of frustration, but he knew he needed to snap out of it. His pulse racing, he stood up and rushed to find the attendant.

"I need to report a missing person,

immediately, to the police. How do I do this?"

"Winnipeg's the next station. It's about fifteen minutes away. We'll stop there for half an hour. I can take you to the office where they'll help you. In fact, I'll make a short report and radio ahead about the situation."

Nigel collapsed into his seat in sheer disbelief at his predicament. It struck him that, as usual, he'd only had a peripheral understanding of the trip, aware only of the basic facts. He sighed. He hadn't bothered to even look at the train ticket Kevy had handed him as they boarded the train in Toronto.

"Here," she'd said, "keep your ticket in your wallet in case a ticket inspector should ask to see it," and he'd simply pocketed it.

Inspector Emery at the Winnipeg railway police station appeared informed, polite, and empathetic. "Mr. Paul, we have a report here from the Thunder Bay police station where your wife presented herself, asked the police to expect a missing persons report on her, and told them to ignore it. She has assured the police she'd safe, and her message to you is not to look for her."

"Is that all?" he asked, embarrassed.

"Mr. Paul, we're convinced nothing illegal or suspicious has happened. There's no coercion or anything like it involved. A sane and sound person willfully walked away from a train. This is not a police matter anymore. I am so sorry, and I wish both of you the best."

Realization dawned upon Nigel that he had to handle the problem to determine what had happened and what to do next. As the train gathered speed toward Edmonton, its final destination, he tried to collect his wits as he settled back in his seat. Outside, a beautiful day had dawned. He looked up into a cloudless blue sky, brilliant golden sunshine pouring into the coach and his misery deepened.

He looked up at the baggage rack above his seat and brought down his carry-on travel bag—which, as usual, had been packed by Kevina. He rummaged through the bag looking for any clues that might shed a light on his present situation. He found an envelope, addressed simply: *Nigel*. There was a tremor in his hands and his pulse quickened as he opened the envelope and unfolded the single page in Kevy's unmistakable handwriting.

*Nigel,*

*After a lot of soul-searching, I came to the conclusion that our paths have diverged, and we have drifted apart, irreconcilably. I tried to discuss our situation with you several times, but you were not responsive. The feeling you once had for me has been dead for a long time. This simple fact has been in my face for the last decade or so.*

*We have reached the end of our journey together. I have finally left you.*

*I will be safe, so do not worry about my safety. Please do not look for me—I will not be reachable. I have resigned from my job, as well.*

*All the arrangements for this trip are in place. In Edmonton, take the taxi to the nearby Holiday Inn Express where there is a confirmed reservation for you. Sam and Cheryl will meet you at the Holiday Inn in the bar.*

*All is taken care of at home and the bank, as well. Some important points of contact and notes are listed overleaf. I have taken nothing, and I do not wish to take anything from you. I will be overseas for a while and will contact you when I return in about six months, and we can settle our affairs then.*

*Kevina*

That was definitely Kevy—straightforward and to the point, no theatrics, and no expression of emotion. And yet he could feel her reluctance and considerable deliberation she must've felt while writing the letter, tears in her eyes. She would know the impact her unexpected departure would have on him, but he also knew that she could be quite tough.

Nigel was overcome with an unease and discomfort unlike any he had ever felt before. She was right: he had indeed made a habit of not paying any attention to her. When was it he'd last had a discussion with her on any subject? They were like two interlocked wheels, moving well in unison, but only mechanically—doing exactly what was required, devoid of any emotion. There were no tender moments between them.

When had he last shared a joke with her? She used to tell him stories from her work and travels. He remembered that while narrating humorous office situations involving her office colleagues, Kevina always found a positive angle. Over the years, his merriment at her stories had withered into mirthless grunts and finally into stares of boredom. Of late, she hardly ever mentioned her office, and he never asked about it.

Yes, she was right: they'd become two beings existing physically close but far apart in every other level. He'd indeed become blind, though knew that every marriage required continued nurturing.

Kevina had taken almost half a year to plan what in her mind she'd called her Escape From Nigel. After three decades with him, she'd convinced herself she had to make a choice between two alternatives: one was to continue as she had over the years with him, where life had slowed to his pace; the other was to move on to another plane in life.

It was not as if she were dumping him. No, she'd tried to discuss the subject of change with him on several occasions, but he'd dismissed it out of hand and ended the discussion immediately. She interpreted this stance as a clear signal that his level of concern for her had diminished beyond the point of no return. He hardly knew what she did at work except to know that she had a very senior, well-paid position. They had little to share except the material possessions around them, with no sentimentality accompanying it. The flame of love and passion had dimmed over the years, finally extinguishing itself some time ago. She remembered the first time she seriously thought about the possibility of leaving him.

She had gone to London International Airport, about two hundred kilometers west of Toronto, one Sunday morning in late May. There was a light, southerly breeze, an early harbinger of the warm summer to come. The birds were celebrating with their incessant tweeting and flying about in amorphous formations as if to show their superior flexibility over the man-made machines. It was a beautiful day to fly, dwell on life, and take stock of her situation.

She completed her preflight check around the single turbine engine Saturn. The Saturn was a marvel of modern science and engineering, an all-composite aircraft with onboard electronics, called the e-cockpit. As she fired the engine up, she noticed the electronic aircraft management system (EAMS) had adjusted the engine's parameters for taxiing. The EAMS monitored the engine's status and configured it for the different phases of flight.

She settled into the cozy interior; the seats had been engineered to wrap comfortably around the human body. The EAMS also automatically communicated with the air traffic management system, and she saw the air traffic clearance flash on her screen.

She took off and headed northbound, handling the aircraft effortlessly, as if it were second nature. Her entire itinerary for the next two hours had been programmed into the EAMS. All she had to do was monitor the aircraft and watch as the world unfolded beneath her. She felt detached from the world, as if she were a mere spectator to the earthly events. Flying gave her such a feeling of euphoria, she found it relaxing—she was at peace with herself and in harmony with the surrounding nature, a time to reach deep into her soul. It was a feeling only other aviators were able to understand.

She had tried several times to convince Nigel to go up with her, telling him how beautiful the day was, wanting to acquaint him with the breathtaking beauty of Ontario from the air, to show him the heavenly sight that would appear beneath them. He'd always dismiss the topic of flying with a grunt, muttering something like, "We've done that before, and I have stuff to do today."

To be fair, he never showed any resentment toward her hobby, or any of her other passions, for that matter, such as working out or playing tennis. He just never showed any interest at all. Was it deliberate on his part to give her her own space, or was it simply another manifestation of his continued lack of interest in her, what she did, what she thought, or who she was?

They'd shared the same space-time dimension but were worlds apart in the fifth dimension, that of shared emotions. Over time, Kevina attributed Nigel's changed attitude as a casualty of the advancing tide of age, because he hadn't always been like that.

She remembered the first time she'd met him at a soiree at a friend's house almost forty years earlier. He'd come across as an engaging, well-read, financial professional, and they'd hit it off, quite well. In many ways, he seemed to complement her, when it came to her interests and capabilities. While she was a great technocrat who was quite meticulous in the technical arena, and though she had a good understanding of financial matters—especially when it came to costing out proposals for customers—she was always grateful her finance department was there to put the numbers together. Numbers, especially those related to accounting matters, had always bored her, and she was glad Nigel was at ease with them.

In the early years of their wedded life, Nigel had managed their investments and always surprised Kevina with his financial analysis. She quickly recognized that he was a numbers guy, someone who could recall facts and anecdotes from his wide reading. She had really enjoyed learning a lot from him and that aspect of his life.

They were never overly expressive types. Rather, they enjoyed their relationship in quietude, knowing that each was there for the other. They'd go for long walks and spend a lot of time reading and discussing books and magazine articles. Kevina remembered the good times they'd shared, strolling arm in arm along the nature trails in the vicinity of their home. She'd talk about the birds and the flowers, and he'd listen with amazement at her knowledge on those subjects. Almost by design, they avoided long, in-depth discussions about their work, which was therapeutic, as they'd discarded issues related to work outside the door to their house.

Nigel was never a romantic. He was more down to earth, though off and on, he'd surprise her with simple gifts which showed he'd given the matter some thought before purchasing the items. He did not like surprises himself, but that was then. A lot had changed—and mostly for the worse, as far as Kevina was concerned.

A short while back, Nigel had surprised her by suggesting the two of them should take a train holiday to the Rockies in the late summer. The sense of elation from the surprise was short-lived, however, when she discovered that his real motive was to meet up with some longtime friends. They could not undertake the trip that year because of their daughter's sickness and finally her death, but a year or so later, Nigel raised the subject of the trip again.

At about four thousand feet, somewhere a hundred miles west of Toronto, it struck Kevina that the proposed train trip offered her the opportunity to explore her escape options. He, as usual, would expect her to organize the full trip. She knew he trusted her completely. Their house was paid for, as was their cottage near Goodrich, west of Toronto. They had no debts, and their savings in bonds and stocks had survived the market vicissitudes of earlier, uncertain times reasonably well—no small thanks to Kevina's wise, and at times lucky, investment decisions. She also paid all the bills and managed all their bank accounts, which were in their joint names.

She knew Nigel well enough to predict that once he was over the initial shock of the new wrinkle in his life, he'd adjust and settle down, especially when he realized she'd planned it so as to have minimal impact upon his material world. She sighed at the thought that she'd ceased to be a factor in his life at the sentimental level. And it was not as if he was incapable of emotion—not at all.

She'd seen him with their daughter and was keenly aware of the closeness between them, particularly during Shelly's final days. She felt that his love for Shelly was profound and exquisite, indeed. His love sustained Shelly and kept her spirits high. Kevina was convinced he gave her that inner strength to initially fight the disease, and finally, to accept the inevitable.

Shelly had asked, looking directly at her dad, "Will I see you in heaven?" It was a crushing moment. Kevina had seen tears well up in his eyes, and she'd touched his hand to support him, though she had not been able to contain her own tears. Shelly added, "I had the best parents in the world, and now I have to go. I'm not scared anymore. I know I'll see you again, perhaps in heaven, or in my next life." She then drifted into sleep, overcome by the painkillers she'd been taking.

Kevina had always been struck by Shelly's wisdom and her adult-like maturity, which she'd acquired at an early age. She passed away early the next morning, and Nigel had broken down completely. He took a long time to recover his composure. For a long time after, his voice cracked at any remembrance of Shelly. Kevina couldn't contain her own tears of grief and barely managed to maintain her own composure.

With Shelly's departure, the already weakened emotional bridge between Kevina and Nigel collapsed, though they maintained civility toward each other, and hardly ever fought.

The chasm between them deepened. Strangely, Nigel seemed comfortable, but inside Kevina, there was an ever-widening void. She felt there needed to be a fundamental change between them.

Kevina was totally in her element when it came to planning her escape from what she privately called her Wedlock Prison, her loveless castle of material warmth and comfort that was otherwise empty and emotionally icy cold. She quietly but resolutely put together a detailed plan to escape from her current predicament where she'd experienced deep loneliness in the close proximity of her companion.

For him to sleep through a long flight or a long car journey was no problem. In fact, she viewed his ability to turn his mind off and succumb to deep slumber at will with envy. She was exactly the opposite herself—she hardly ever slept in her travels, regardless of the duration or the comfort. Thunder Bay, the midway point between Toronto and Edmonton, more or less, there would be the perfect opportunity for her to slip out. She was virtually certain Nigel would not even notice her departure until breakfast time the following morning, as the train was approaching Edmonton.

Professionally, she could simply quit her job; she was already eligible for early retirement. Even though it meant a somewhat reduced pension, initially, it was quite comfortable, and she would be free to do consulting work as long as it didn't conflict with C-Systems' company business.

To resign from her company, her legal obligation was to give the company a two-month notice or forfeit equivalent salary. She'd planned it perfectly. She had a fairly lengthy backlog of unused leave, and she offered it to them without any recompense to her, along with a cheque for two months' salary. Her parting generosity was an indication of the gratitude she felt toward her company. As the chief technology officer, she had an impeccable record of accomplishments. She was also recognized as a superb manager and someone who was had been ahead in succession planning for her own position. She'd already mentored two bright, energetic, and relatively young candidates. Then, one evening—quite unceremoniously—she walked out. Only her closest business associates in and out of the company had been aware of her plans. She decided to leave a short note for her colleagues:

*I thank the company for the wonderful twenty-two years of employment and opportunity. My decision to resign is sudden and effective immediately. I have cleared all the formalities with our accounting department. My reasons for leaving are very personal, and I will not be looking for employment in the future, though I may do some consulting work without causing any conflict with the company business.*

*I am leaving with nothing that is company property. Sandra and Dave will be able to run the department without any difficulty. I thank my colleagues for what I have learned from them, and I am grateful for the opportunities provided to me to grow with the company. For those who may want to contact me for any reason, our HR department will have my contact details.*

*I wish you all success and good health.*

*Kevina Paul*

On the home front, she'd written instructions and information about their bank accounts for Nigel on a single page. All of the regular household bills were being paid automatically from the account, however, she'd left the names and phone numbers of her contacts, should he need them. She'd removed her name from Nigel's bank account to assure Nigel that she'd no longer be able to access it.

It was in the fall that year, when, one morning, they'd left together in a taxi for the train station, boarded the train uneventfully, and Nigel, of course, had been totally unaware of her plan. She'd selected Thunder Bay because it was where they'd arrive at about 2:00 a.m. Her final communication to him—her parting note—was short, emotionless, and to the point.

# 3

She knew she was just a few minutes away from the next station, Thunder Bay. Nigel was dozing. Everything was set. She'd soon be gone from his life. This was a big moment, but she handled it routinely with the precision and efficiency she was used to in the execution of her professional duties. She was about to walk out on her life partner, and she felt no emotion. Well, perhaps there was a twinge of guilt. She hesitated momentarily, but this was a now or never moment.

She gave him one last look and walked out from the train, her carry-on bag rolling behind her. Outside the train station, she felt the cool autumn wind upon her face. Winter was just around the corner, but she was headed for somewhere warm—much warmer. She hailed a cab, and stopped at the police station, en route to the airport.

Inside, she asked to speak to the duty officer who greeted her saying, "Inspector Sam McCurdy, ma'am. What can I do for you?"

She cleared her throat and began, "I have a rather unusual report and request to make. First, I want to tell you that you will very likely receive a lost persons report about me, most likely from my husband. I request that you tell the person reporting that I am completely safe, of sound mind, and have deliberately and willfully walked out on my husband. Also, let me assure you that I am under no external compulsion of any sort. My actions are totally self-willed. I can tell you all about myself, my full contact data, exactly where I'm going, and what I'm doing, but in total confidence, please. So there's no missing person issue at all—just the breakup of a marriage, of no interest to the police, or anyone else, for that matter. It is a domestic affair."

"Please sit down, ma'am. Would you like a coffee or a glass of water? First, let me ask you: are you all right?" After noting her affirmative nods, he continued, "I will have to file a report, take all your data, and convince myself you are under no inappropriate external pressure from anyone and are doing this completely on your own. Let's begin with this form."

A few minutes later, the police officer seemed quite satisfied and bade her good-bye. He gave her his phone number and e-mail address and asked her to stay in touch.

She got back into the taxi. At the airport, she boarded a short connecting flight to Chicago. By mid-afternoon, she found herself in a business-class seat on the latest supersonic cruiser aircraft to Montego Bay, Jamaica.

She checked her e-mail from her seat. She checked her voice mail as well—all voice mail messages, both on her cell phone and home phone, had been converted to digital form and delivered automatically to her e-mail account. During the flight, she declined any offers of food or drink except for a glass of water. After an hour or so, the pilot announced that they'd be landing at Montego Bay International Airport in Jamaica within the next few minutes.

The aircraft made an approach over the Caribbean Sea. The greenish blue of the sea was the same color as Shelly's eyes. Shelly had told her once, before her illness, "I want to go around the world with you, Mom. I want to see the tropics and faraway lands," but the hands of fate did not permit her dream to come true.

Kevina boarded the bus for the Sun Hotel Resort.

"Madam, are you attending the aviation conference?" the driver asked.

When she nodded, the driver asked her name and said, "Let me welcome you. Here is a package with all that you need for the conference, which will begin at 8:00 a.m. sharp, with breakfast."

At the Sun Hotel, the receptionist greeted her and said, "Ah, Ms. Paul, we have the executive suite ready for you. The porter will show you to your room. You're also invited to a preconference icebreaker in Manley Hall at 7:00 p.m."

She quickly freshened up in her room, and sat there, alone, mulling over what she'd done.

How will Nigel react?

Definitely not good immediately—he'd be devastated for sure. First, he'd experience disbelief, and she knew it would take some time for him to come out of it. But he *would* recover. At least, that's what she'd hoped. Had her hope simply been a way to justify her sudden action?

Tears welled up in her eyes, and she knew she had to find a way to distract herself. She immediately proceeded to the icebreaker, downstairs in the big hall.

She walked into the hall a few minutes before 8:00 p.m., where her attention was, at once, arrested by a figure on the stage. The audience was mostly standing, chit-chatting, and nursing drinks. Some of them appeared to be enjoying listening to the man on the stage.

She heard, "We all know that long, long ago, we were monkeys—all of us. Well, Charles Darwin told us that. Yeah, man. How did we change from monkeys to humans? Mind you, I'm not entirely convinced this was a good idea at all—we were so happy monkeying around—but let me tell you what probably happened. One day, about a million years ago, two monkeys were walking together somewhere in central Africa. That was when one monkey turned to the other and said, 'Don't you ever call me a monkey again.'

"'Why not? That is what we are.'

"'Well, from now on, I am no more a monkey; I am a Homo erectus.'

"This was a historic moment, but you will not find it in any book on Anthropology. Of course, ladies and gentlemen, in reality, this particular conversation couldn't have taken place then, because language had not been invented yet. For that to happen, humans had to wait for several hundreds of thousand years. Yeah, man."

Her mind strayed away from the budding comedian. He had a good delivery, though. She recognized a group near the bar, well out of range of the comedian's voice. She made her way over and ordered a glass of red wine.

"Kay," she heard from behind her, the voice

addressing her by what people generally called her in professional settings. "Kay, we were just talking about you."

She recognized the distinct Jamaican accent of Stub Phillipson, someone she'd known for several years. Stub was the president of the Inter-Caribbean Air Traffic Management Agency, the recently formed, multinational agency of all the Caribbean nations, overseeing the provision of air traffic control services to all aircraft flying in the Caribbean region.

"And what were you saying about me? Something good, I hope."

"Of course. We're looking forward to your keynote talk on the threats facing global air traffic management and security measures."

"Ah, Stub, you seem well prepared. I know you're chairing the conference," she said with a warm smile.

After a couple of warm handshakes, a bit of small talk over a glass of red wine, and half a sandwich, the evening wore to a close.

Back in her room, she had to try not to think about Nigel.

She reviewed her speech. She was going to talk about the vulnerability of the global aviation system to sabotage from within the next day—cyber-terrorism in aviation at a global scale. That was what they were expecting, but she knew that during her presentation, she must remain at the top level of the subject, and not sink into the depth of details.

Later, she meditated for about twenty minutes and felt relaxed. She turned off the lights and willed herself to fall asleep.

* * *

The next morning, she was at her eloquent best, and words flowed out of her like spring water pouring out of a mountainside—crisp and fresh with new ideas. Her words, which revealed her clear and authoritative grasp of the subject matter, were delivered with perfect intonation. She intuitively knew when to pause, survey the audience, and carry on. She knew the power of silence in a speech and felt that it was in those silences that there was real contact with each member of the audience on an individual basis. There was pin-drop silence during her presentation, and there were no questions even though many in the audience took copious notes. She knew there would be a lot of follow-up and one-on-one discussions.

The hour assigned to her was over in a flash. The moderator, aware of the impact she'd had on the audience, hadn't sent any signals for her to hurry up as he'd done before with many a rambling, boring delivery, where the audience and the speaker were on completely different frequencies. This was far from the case with Dr. Paul's presentation that morning.

After a brief introduction of her main topic, she arrived quickly at the key point of her speech: "As we all know today, the threat of cyber-warfare is already upon us. International agencies have done a great job of developing and convincing most member nations to implement adequate controls over viruses. As well, cyber-security agencies have developed anti-virus capabilities that are able to identify, isolate, and disable such malicious software.

"Let me remind you of what happened in the Middle East: many of you may be aware of the Stuxnet virus, which was developed and deployed around the end of the first decade of this century. It has been said that this was the first launch of cyber-warfare, which was, in fact, a cyber-attack. Stuxnet was a very efficient software worm that was introduced remotely into the supervisory control and data acquisition systems of certain nuclear-enrichment plants. First, the main plant was surreptitiously infected and successfully disabled. The worm then went on to replicate itself, quickly infiltrating multiple associated sites. The worm penetrated and disrupted their operating systems, causing huge malfunctions in multiple associated sites. Thus, a much-feared plan to develop nuclear weapons was thwarted."

Kevina knew this was about all she could say because many strongly believed Stuxnet had been conceived by the United States to disable the nuclear warfare capabilities of a then-hostile Iran. Though Iran, the United States, and other Western nations currently enjoyed friendly relationships, she also knew that a few people had been opposed to the détente, and she didn't dwell on the history any further.

She continued, "It is believed, however, that Stuxnet led to the proliferation of similar malware. Since then, defense department software experts in many countries have been working hard to fight and neutralize destructive software worms like Duqu, Gauss, and so on. Over the past few decades, we've heard a lot about cyber-attacks on our financial, corporate, personal, and occasionally, government systems, but so far, we have not heard about an attack on aviation systems.

"What I'm saying is there are numerous and compelling reasons to strengthen the robustness of our critical systems, and air traffic management systems are certainly one of those. The safety, security, economic, and even the political implications of disrupted ATM systems are huge and widespread. I urge the member nations that we invest heavily to enhance the capabilities of our regional and global ATM systems to increase their safety, capacity, and efficiency. It is very important that we do everything we can to make our systems as secure as possible. The price for no action will be huge and unaffordable."

Over coffee break, and then again over lunch, she was besieged by several conference attendees who solicited her views on the safeguards needed to protect the global system from sabotage from within. She explained that since the system was "kind of closed" and not accessible to the general public, there was no great danger posed by ordinary hackers. The threat of jamming GPS satellites had significantly diminished. Considerable effort had been expended to make the overall system resistant to jamming by amateurs. The focus of aviation authorities had been to reduce the vulnerability of the GPS-dependent global air traffic management system from external threats, and to be fair, the measures had collectively succeeded in enhancing the security.

She, however, had wanted to focus on the threats from within the system by sophisticated terrorists who posed as legitimate users of the system. And there was no shortage of terrorists, who were very knowledgeable about the aviation infrastructure who were trained in the use of the latest technology.

In the global air traffic management system, computers on the ground communicated with computers in the air. Most of the frequencies over which the communications took place used satellites and were not easily accessible to the public or to common hackers. Additionally, all aircraft had unique identification codes combined with data encryption, which provided another layer of protection from a hacker on the outside.

She continued to elaborate on her theme from earlier on the podium, that a virus or destructive program could be deliberately sent from a seemingly normal aircraft, flying within an airspace, after the aircraft had established legitimate communication with the ground ATM computers. Depending on the sophistication of the virus, the entire global system could be disrupted.

One way to implement measures to prevent successful attempts by saboteurs was for the aviation authorities and the manufacturers of airborne and ground systems to cooperate. She said that the best minds in the aviation industry must come together to identify every possible terrorism scenario, and then ensure that a layer of security was in place to thwart each such attempt.

As the shadows outside the conference hall lengthened, and as her vocal cords began to reveal a tired hoarseness due to almost non-stop talking, she slid away early from the evening cocktail, taking refuge in the deserted but reasonably equipped gym in the hotel basement. She jogged and walked briskly on the treadmill for about an hour. By the time the meter on the machine said she'd expended over five hundred calories, she was panting. Walking toward the steam room and shower, she felt mentally relaxed and surprisingly rejuvenated.

She looked at herself in the mirror in the steam room with satisfaction. She looked lean and athletic, and she knew she'd kept the forces of advancing age at bay. She was happy in her skin in that respect. Her recipe for combating aging was simple—regular exercise, simple dietary habits, engaging her mind with challenging issues, lots of reading, and yes, regular meditation.

She spread her towel, sat down, and meditated in the steam room, relaxing every muscle in her body, her mind becoming still as she ceased thinking about anything in particular for a few minutes. A tingling sensation spread throughout her body.

Slowly, her mind emerged from her meditative stance. She'd been able to shut off her thoughts about Nigel for much of the day.

She showered quickly and was quite hungry when she reached her room, having realized she'd hardly eaten during the day.

Of the several restaurants in the hotel, she chose to dine in the Japanese restaurant by herself. Luckily, the restaurant wasn't busy as all of the attendees were still at the evening social that would, no doubt, stretch well into the night, and perhaps into the early morning hours. She needed time to think.

Deep from the recesses of her mind, as it did so often lately, Shelly's face took shape, and she recalled her last few days in the world.

"Mom, you know I won't be around for much longer," Shelly had said.

"Darling, you must not say that or even think such thoughts. The doctors and modern science, together, are fighting for you. You need to help them by thinking positive thoughts and not give up so quickly. They need your help so that you can come out of this. I know you can, honey."

"I used to think that for a long time, but now I hear God calling. In the normal order of things, I should have outlived you all, but that's not my reality."

Where was she getting these ideas from? What was the source of this spiritual wisdom?

"Mom, the time for me to depart this world has come."

Kevina swallowed hard at what she was hearing as she searched for appropriate words to respond.

Shelly continued, "I know you don't know what to say to me, but accept what I'm saying because it's the truth. The doctors have called my illness terminal. I'm not afraid anymore. I'm ready to begin another journey into another life."

Shelly had leukemia, which often strikes children, and this was acute lymphoblastic leukemia which had proven deadly for Shelly, who was an unusually intelligent and perceptive child. Kevina used to say to her friends and relatives, only a year or so earlier that Shelly was five, going on forty.

Tears welled up in her eyes. Drop after drop rolled down her cheeks and into her sushi platter.

She thought of Nigel and wondered whether she'd done the right thing the previous day, only a short year after Shelly's death. She could easily call Nigel and tell him she was coming back to him. She knew he'd instantly and genuinely welcome that, but she had to be absolutely sure she was not thrust back to square one a short period after their reconciliation.

How might she feel then?

She'd already made the break, and she was determined to continue with it. He had to make the first move now, and she had to wait for it.

Her reverie was interrupted when a familiar voice yanked her back to the reality of the restaurant. She cleared her throat and forced a rather fake smile, hoping her tears weren't noticeable.

Kevina looked up and recognized the big Adam's apple beneath a thin face that was losing the war against the onslaught of advancing age. She'd have had difficulty recognizing the face, but the prominent Adam's apple brought into focus the moment and the place she'd last met the man.

It was about ten years earlier in Tehran, Iran, that she'd first met Claude—his last name momentarily eluded her. Claude was the president of a local, high-technology company that had collaborated with Kevina's company, C Systems. C Systems was under a multi-million-dollar contract to build a regional military defense system. Relations between Iran and the West had improved, and C Systems had provided a modern electronic surveillance system for national and regional defense, counter-terrorism, and drug interdiction.

"Hello, Claude. It's been a long time." She greeted him with a touch of insincerity, trying hard not to focus on his neck.

"Kay, that was a great presentation this morning. I thoroughly enjoyed it. You touched upon the very subject we're really concerned with. How are you, by the way? You haven't changed at all. You still look beautiful, Kay!"

"Thanks, Claude. You look good, as well." She felt compelled to lie—there was really no other option but to do so. She hoped she sounded sincere.

"You know, back in Tehran, I still tell the boys that no one knows our system better than Dr. Paul of C Systems. We want you to visit us so we can talk about enhancements."

"Well, Claude, things have changed. You should know that I am no longer with C Systems."

"Have you gone over to the competition? Which one?"

"No, Claude, I'm on my own—not with any company."

A contemplative silence fell over Claude as he appeared to digest the information.

"May I sit down? I know you've finished dinner; maybe I can order coffee for both of us."

Kevina felt a bit trapped. "Claude, I'm a bit tired today, and I know I have to get back early and rest up. Tomorrow will be a busy day, but I guess we can have a quick coffee. Tea, in my case—herbal tea, please."

He ordered coffee, and she had a cup of herbal tea. After a few minutes, he broke through the small talk and said, "Look, Kay, you could be of great use to my company, and I'm sure the company would like to hire you as a consultant. We'll pay you a retainer, a per diem, and all of the expenses— first class. I'll talk to Tehran tonight and e-mail you a draft contract for your review, first thing tomorrow. Please think about this. It doesn't stop you from doing anything else you want to pursue in your career."

"Thanks, Claude, but this is all a bit too sudden. I'll have to think this over and let you know." She signed the bill over to her room, got up, shook his hand, and walked out.

She remembered he was a man she never particularly liked, a man she felt could not be trusted, though she'd always maintained professional courtesies with him. And, as luck would have it, he was a man making her an interesting offer regarding a subject that she'd thought about extensively. She knew she had great ideas that could help move them toward the South Asia defense system, which involved several nations who were trying to fight terrorism and drug trafficking. Her mind wavered between two scenarios—one of mistrust toward him and the other which was the opportunity he presented. The scenarios were at odds with each other.

She quickened her pace toward her room. She tried to stop thinking about the meeting, but then her thoughts diverted to Nigel.

Nigel should be in Edmonton, meeting their friends. She had confidence in his ability to find a new comfort zone, but she also knew that, deep down, he'd miss her, just as she oddly missed him at that very moment.

She meditated in her room for about twenty minutes. Detached from reality, she felt at one with the world beyond, and a sense of contentment enveloped her. She switched off the light—and with that, amazingly, her consciousness—and fell asleep.

Kevina got up just a few minutes before the alarm as she almost always did. She muttered a voice command to her computer which cancelled the wake-up alarm. The computer had already collected her e-mail and announced that she had five e-mails, but none of them from Nigel. Four of them were from her office. She skipped them all, thinking she'd address them later.

The fifth e-mail was from Claude. The computer read the first couple of lines aloud.

"Good morning, Kevina. It was good to talk to you last night. Attached is a summary of the highlights of the offer that will be sent to you by the end of the day. You will see me during the day at one of the sessions, where I hope to get some reaction from you."

Kevina ordered the computer to standby. During her shower, she reached a decision: she would seriously consider Claude's offer. She had nothing to lose. She'd have to evaluate the time required. She was wary of Claude, but she'd be willing to take the risk. She had the confidence that she'd be able to handle both him and the assignment.

She'd visited Iran several times and had come to appreciate its rich history and culture. She remembered the beautiful city of Isfahan. It was there she'd first met Claude, when she was on a tour of the churches in the city. Half-way through the tour, she'd become aware of a guy with a prominent Adam's apple who was trying to catch her eye. He finally walked up to her.

The Adam's apple said, "Dr. Paul, I was in the room during your presentation at the air force HQ in Tehran on the command and control system. It was very impressive. My company is the designated corporate partner of the air force and gets involved with all air force foreign contracts. I'm Claude Harazi, the CEO. Here's my card."

"Nice to meet you, Mr. Harazi. I'll ask our marketing VP to get in touch with you immediately."

That night, she'd made her marketing department aware of Claude, and within a few days, the company marketing VP had told her that Claude's company had been signed on as the local partner. About two years later—and after several visits by Kevina and her company's technical and senior officials— reciprocal visits by the South Asian Alliance staff, and a long, drawn-out bidding process, a multi-million-dollar contract had finally been signed. The contract had been well supported by the new North Atlantic Alliance.

During the execution of the contract, Kevina had met with Claude several times. At times, it appeared as though he had two agendas—the obvious and public one, and a hidden, private one. But as fate would have it, she was about to enter into a business relationship with him. She resolved to conquer her discomfort because the challenge was attractive. She felt that she should give it a chance and let a professional relationship develop between them. One aspect of Claude that she had to acknowledge was that her previous association with him had been successful for C Systems, and hence, for Kevina, as well.

She stepped out of her room and commenced her walk to the conference hall. The tropical sun bathed the landscape as a light breeze swept across the resort. Birds, excitedly twittering away, greeted the dawn of yet another lovely day. She took the slightly longer route so she could go to the beach to listen to the hypnotic, incessant crashing of the waves on the sand that she found so soothing.

She stopped and looked into the horizon where the sky met the ocean before venturing into the hall. Claude was waiting there for her. "Well,

Dr. Paul, did you get time to see my preliminary e-mail?" he said.

"I'm considering it, but you'll have to tell me a lot more about it."

Claude said that he'd spoken to his head office and that he was ready to discuss the details. He wanted Kevina to examine the vulnerability of the national and regional ATM systems—and even the defence system—to terrorism, and participate in the development and implementation of measures to protect it. Kevina was interested in knowing what the limitations were, to whom she would report, and whether the Iranian government was fully supportive of the initiative. She was assured of a free hand in defining the study and its timetable, and cost seemed not to be an issue—within reason. She could set her own agenda within the overall guidelines and be accountable to him. The government was aware and supportive and had identified the need to enhance the robustness of the total system as a top priority.

Before Kevina could ask, Claude emphasized, "Yes, Vice President Zakir Tandorost is fully behind the project and will be very pleased to meet you in Tehran as soon as you are able to go there."

She smiled at the mention of Zakir's name, the VP of Iran's Civil-Military Aviation Organization. She'd known him for over a decade. He'd been the overall architect of the system, of course, along with her.

That evening, the draft contract arrived in her in-box. Kevina reviewed it and deemed it fully acceptable. Claude had wisely used the consultant contract template from C Systems, which was quite familiar to her. Kevina was quite comforted when she noticed she had the option of backing out of the contract after her initial visit to Tehran. With that escape clause, she knew she'd sign the contract immediately.

A day later, Kevina was on a flight from Kingston to London, and from there, to catch a flight to Tehran. The flight proceeded uneventfully. Kevina relaxed, sipped some wine, and mostly, as she always did, nibbled on the food. On the London-to-Tehran flight, the relatively new sonic cruiser aircraft flew at just below the speed of sound. Direct routing combined with a favorable tailwind to shorten the flight by almost two hours. The monotone whirring of the engines and suspended tranquility had a hypnotic effect. For a while, her whole body seemed elevated and floating, her heartbeat settled down to about fifty beats per minute, and she felt totally rejuvenated in mind, body, and spirit.

She remembered the words of her meditation guru, even though his name had faded from her memory: "Anyone can learn to meditate; it's doing it regularly that's the problem. Three simple sentences will tell you about meditation: inhale slowly, using your diaphragm above your abdomen to fill your lungs; hold it for some time; exhale slowly. Repeat for twenty minutes, daily. You, like the vast majority of others, will find it hard to set aside the mere fifteen minutes a day to meditate. But if you do it right, it will transform you in a total sense."

"How will I know when I am doing it right?" she had asked.

"That, my dear, is the amazing thing about meditation: you will simply know when you're doing it right. No one will need to tell you, you'll just know it...you will know it...know it." The words receded into another temporal dimension, and she fell into a comfortable slumber.

The next thing she knew, the aircraft had made a smooth landing at Tehran Imam Khomeini International Airport.

# 4

Surin was in his car when he got a call from Claude in Tehran. This was one time he wished his driver was behind the wheel and he, simply a passenger. Normally, he preferred to drive his smart car, as he knew how—and more importantly, when—to use the car's e-mode. This was the relatively new automated feature in the e-car.

Surin pulled over and said loudly, "Hello, Claude. What's up?" He had to raise his voice because, despite the vehicle's noise-suppression capabilities which kept the inside of the car as quiet as possible, the noise of the traffic was deafening. The incessant honking was—as it always had been— the typical, signature tune, as it were, on the streets of Bengaluru, and for that matter, of many cities in South Asia. Each honk conveyed a single message: "Hey, get out of my way—now!"

"Hi, Surin. Good morning. It seems you're on your way to work, am I right?"

"Yes, it's very noisy. I can just barely hear you. Go ahead, please."

"Okay, let me come to the point of this call: I'm bidding for an approved top-secret software development program in civil-military aviation and would like you, in particular, to work with us on an exclusive basis, as you've done in the past. What do you say? If you agree, even in principle, I can send all the background info for you to review and then confirm your response with me."

"Thanks, for thinking of me, Claude, but remember that the last time we worked with you it was actually my company, GS Systems, that had the contract with you, and I was simply GS's designated principal. If I worked with you again, it would have to be the same arrangement—I can only work with you as a part of GS."

He wanted to ensure no misunderstanding on Claude's part, up front. GS was his employer, and Surin liked having the GS umbrella over him. He knew that the company had a great reputation for its achievements, and more importantly, for its commitment to ethics. That way, GS kept its employees out of trouble in several countries, which had become very important of late. The downside of the growth and the advancement in information technology was that it was available to all users—the legitimate as well as the crooks and terrorists. The ubiquity of the Internet was such that it provided access to anyone, anywhere. It had become a double-edged sword, nearly impossible to control, or even fully monitor, given its anyone-anywhere characteristic. Many countries were spending a lot of money developing Internet monitoring capabilities, and they were being lambasted from all sides, accused of violating personal freedoms, spying on its own citizens, and so on. Personally, Surin had never felt threatened by legitimate governments of democratic nations conducting surveillance for enhancing the security of its citizens and their property. In fact, he had participated in developing such specialized software to keep an eye on social media and look for tips on illegal and destructive activities of criminal minds. There was also the issue of age-old practices of corruption in South Asian countries, and GS had a well-recognized reputation for being a clean company that did not tolerate improper dealings within the company and with external agencies.

"Of course. That's what I meant. Please discuss this with your company and get back to me, ASAP."

"Okay, I'll get back to you within a couple of days." He hung up.

Surin was quite pleased with this development. He liked Iran and was quite pleased with its political evolution as a forward-looking country. He sent a quick, short e-mail to his company, outlining what Claude had proposed.

Shortly after, GS Systems sent a draft contract to Claude to get the ball rolling.

In the draft contract, Claude noticed that Surin was the lead from the GS side. He had a quick meeting with his business manager to put a statement of work in for Surin. For compensation, the previously negotiated fee rate structure was valid. He had this inserted in the contract, signed it, and promptly e-mailed it to Surin for his signature. The contract was finalized within a couple of days.

That day, Claude was particularly pleased that he'd been able to recently enroll two top-notch experts for his project—Dr. Kevina Paul and Mr.

Surin Dev. These two, combined with himself, would make a formidable management team. He called Surin.

"Hey, Surin. How are you?"

"Fine, Claude. I was actually just thinking about you. I'm trying to wrap up my activities here as quickly as I can. When do you want me in Tehran?"

"Actually, I'd like you here, ASAP. Would a week or two be sufficient time to complete your current commitments? It would be convenient if you arrived here on Thursday, a week from now, which actually is the beginning of our weekend, as you know. That way you can take a day to relax, and we can start on our first working day that Saturday."

"Yes, that sounds fine. I'll send you my flight details and so on for pickup at the airport. Where will I be staying?"

"We'll put you up in the Gulf. You've stayed there, before—it's walking distance from the office. Surin, I've some more good news for you. Our advisor-consultant will be Dr. Kevina Paul. I believe you know her from C Systems. She operates now as an independent, technical consultant."

"Wow. Yes, of course, Claude, I remember her well. I really welcome her involvement with us. She's a real pro, indeed, and a pleasure to work with."

"Great, Surin. I'm glad you agree. I'll await your e-mail and look forward to seeing you in about ten days or so. Bye."

Claude was pleased with what he'd achieved, and he basked in the joy of the moment. After a short while, he picked up the phone and dialed a number. When the line was picked up, he said, "All the ducks are lined up. More when I see you."

He waited for a few seconds and then hung up, still smiling.

For Nigel, the Winnipeg-to-Edmonton segment seemed to stretch forever. She must have planned this for some time, without giving him as much as a mere hint. Yes, that was definitely her—a meticulous and thorough planner, whether it was daily chores, holidays, or work.

Did she have another man? No, that was definitely not her style. He knew Kevina was deliberate, not the kind of person to fly off the handle. This was not an error or a spur-of-the-moment reaction to some event. No, this was a meticulously premeditated plan. One side of his mind tried to grapple with a torrent of questions from the other. Why was it that he'd been able to communicate with his daughter so well but not with his wife?

The train continued rolling on, and with time, the storm inside Nigel's mind slowly began to subside as logic came to his rescue. He wondered if, perhaps, the signs weren't there all the while, and he was too self-involved to take notice. He knew that he had, in fact, allowed a wall to be constructed between himself and Kevina. With the passage of time, it had thickened until it became impenetrable. It began to dawn on him that he'd watched it all and had done nothing to stop it. Maybe he'd taken her for granted for too long. She had, in fact, become a piece of furniture: useful, contributing to his overall comfort, but little else. He was aware of Kevina's deep and penetrating intellect, and he began to realize that her actions had been deliberate and firm. He'd have to work very hard and with a lot of conviction to make her change her mind so they'd be able to pick up their lives together.

The storm continued to rage on in his mind.

He looked at her note again, and as he read and reread the words, he started to hear them in her quiet but firm voice. The message was loud and clear that indeed, in her mind, they had reached the end of the line.

By the time the train had pulled into Edmonton, the fact of his present predicament was now fully upon him, that she'd walked out of his life decidedly, unequivocally, and cleanly. He needed to wake up to a new chapter in his life, no question about it. He had also decided he would tell all his close friends and relatives the truth instead of fabricating a lie. She had left him. She was safe, but he didn't know her exact whereabouts. He wondered if she'd discussed her plan to leave him with any of her friends. Could he blame her if she had? Then again, he doubted it; Kevina was a loner at the deepest levels of her psyche.

Nigel hailed a taxi to the Holiday Inn and checked in. Though he was very tired, he couldn't sleep. Sometime in the early morning, he finally succumbed to sleep. The next morning, he stumbled into the bathroom, had a quick shower, and checked voice mail at home, his mobile, and his office, but there was nothing from Kevy, not a peep.

She was really gone.

He went to the hotel lobby bar and awaited his friends.

He found himself reminiscing about their trip to Korea and China almost ten years earlier.

Every minute seemed to have been perfectly planned by Kevina. He remembered how good he'd felt. He just loved it when all he had to do was to move effortlessly, with the flow. Most of the time, he hardly bothered to even know what the next event on the daily agenda was, and he didn't care, because Kevy would have taken care of everything, down to the last minute.

He waited for Sam and Cheryl in the bar/café in the hotel lobby. He sat at the bar and ordered a coffee. When the rather cheery bartender asked how he was, he almost said, "My wife just left me, but other than that, I'm great." Instead, he just faked a smile.

He felt a hand tap his shoulder, and he swiveled around on the bar stool to face a warm and familiar friend.

"Sam, I'm so pleased to see you," Nigel said, and before Sam could ask, he continued, "Kevy's not here. I'll explain. Sit down and let me order..." He couldn't finish the sentence.

"Nigel, we don't have time. Please down your coffee, because Cheryl's waiting outside in the car, traffic's really bad, and we're going to Kevy's and your favorite restaurant—we can all have a drink or two there."

He broke the news of Kevy's departure in the car. He tried to do it calmly, but there was a discernible crackle in his tone. Initial disbelief gave way to grimness.

Without a single interruption, Nigel narrated the events of the previous day in detailed monotone. Nigel wrapped up the narration stating that the authorities had already told him the matter was not theirs to pursue and that it was purely a domestic affair. So now it was a matter that Nigel must handle by himself.

After a brief, contemplative silence, Cheryl posed the inevitable: "Nigel, what will you do now?"

Nigel was unsure, his facial expression betraying his state of perplexity.

Cheryl continued, "Well, Nigel, let me tell you something: you simply cannot let her go—she's a rare gem. We all know she has almost angelic qualities about her, so you need to really think about your next few steps. I really feel she's waiting for your reaction. The first thing we're going to do is to get you out of the hotel, so you won't be alone. We have plenty of room in our house, and you'll be comfortable with us."

Nigel didn't protest as the car swung around back to the Holiday Inn. Inwardly, Nigel had reached a conclusion with respect to his plan, going forward—he had to abort his trip and return home immediately. He knew he was going to devote all of his time and energy to convince Kevina to come back to him, a completely changed man. At the detail level, he wasn't sure what to do.

Sam and Cheryl agreed with his overall plan and wanted to remain close to him to assist in every way they could.

The next day, Nigel found himself airborne on a flight back to Toronto. He remembered their interview with the adoption agency when they'd jointly concluded they should adopt a baby and the immense happiness that followed when the agency had finally found a baby that met their criteria. Kevina and Nigel had both taken six weeks off work to settle in with the baby. As they'd submerged themselves in the daily chores surrounding the upkeep of the baby, Nigel had surprised himself when he'd discovered the fountain of love and dedication he had in his heart. At times, he appeared to be even more motherly than Kevy.

Though Kevy had done the research regarding the nutritional benefits of the various baby foods, it was he who had done most of the feeding and getting up at night. He was almost disappointed when he had to go to work. They'd hired a live-in babysitter, which had worked out well. Kevina, he remembered, had continued to travel, but she did her best to keep in touch, e-mailing voice messages, and through videophone. She seldom missed saying goodnight to Shelly.

Those were such wonderful times.

Then the cruel hand of fate had reached out to deliver a crippling blow. After hearing the diagnosis from the oncologist, Nigel found it hard to remain focused at work. His coworkers had noticed, and he'd been granted a special management leave of three weeks from the office. He'd thought that, during that period of time, he and Kevy had drawn closer to each other—or had it been toward Shelly? Was Shelly the glue that had bound them together, not to each other, but only to herself?

While it seemed that Kevina had deliberately cut all communication links between them and he had no way of communicating with her, he knew that, if she wanted, she could, but she'd wait for a clear signal from him first. He also knew that she could and would wait for as long as was necessary for him to give the first green light.

He was home, now, and for the first time in his life, he felt alone.

He composed a short e-mail to Kevina:

*Dear Kevy,*

*You have awakened me to myself and what I have become, but now I'm ready to change. I want to fill your life with a happiness and contentment that you have not seen with me so far. For that, I'm prepared to do anything that would make you reconsider your decision and come back home.*

*Give me a chance.*

*Forever yours,*

*Nigel*

# 5

The ride from the airport to the Caspian in northern Tehran reacquainted her somewhat with the city she'd known just a few years earlier. That day, as the limo sped toward the hotel, the freshness in the early morning atmosphere had not yet been spoiled by pollution and the noise of the traffic—the curse of Tehran's recent economic prosperity.

Despite the recent construction of overpasses and widening of many of the city's major thoroughfares in the post-sanctions era, the growth in road traffic had continued relentlessly, causing gridlock. Tehran's infrastructure had improved; the roads and the highways, neglected in the years immediately after the revolution, had been generally modernized. A rapid transit system had been commissioned, but despite this, the traffic on the streets was intense. This was the supposed democratic dividend, flowing from the transformation of the political structure of Iranian society from the older theocracy to the newer, more democratic, and development-oriented system. Iran had ushered in a new era of cooperativeness, moderation, and peace in the region. Iran's dynamic and relatively young President Zhiraghi had almost single-handedly created a near miracle in the country, on both domestic and international fronts. His influence on contemporaries in the region had been profound. The resultant flow of foreign investments had, for the most part, created considerable wealth. While the ghosts of the past were still around and manifested their existence on rare occasions, the newer generations of Iranians, both living in and abroad, were concerned more about the promise the future held. President Zhiraghi had succeeded in galvanizing the new generation into a dominant political front. The old guard was isolated, and with the passage of time, it withered into a mere skeleton, generally ineffective but not quite dead. The nation had cautiously risen up from the debris of the authoritarian and extremist regimes of yesteryear. A few more years of Zhiraghi rule and Iran's progress would be unstoppable, or so the political pundits were saying. The pundits had the knack of being wrong often, but on that count, Kevina was inclined to agree with them.

Whether the pillars of democracy were strong enough to withstand the increasingly infrequent—but at times threateningly powerful—gusts of extremist winds was still a matter for time to resolve.

After checking in at the hotel reception, she proceeded to her assigned room. She'd barely stepped in when the phone buzzed, announcing Claude's name.

She had the option of not answering, but she spoke toward the phone anyway. "Good morning, Claude—you're up early."

After exchanging a few pleasantries, Claude

agreed to pick Kevy up at the hotel in a couple of hours, allowing her enough time to freshen up and have a quiet breakfast before the pickup. He said there'd be a full briefing at his office.

"When would I meet with the VP of the JAA?" That was the Joint Aviation Authority of the Middle East, now headquartered in Tehran, Iran.

"The appointment's being arranged. I'll have more on that later in the day, but before the briefing, could we start with your presentation on cyber-terrorism that you gave at the conference a few days ago?"

"Sure. I'm ready for that—it'll be a repeat of what you heard in Jamaica, with some specifics to the situation here. That should be fine for the first day, don't you think?"

"That's fine, Kay. My people haven't heard it. They're really more focused on the issue, and I'm sure they'll have many questions. Don't worry—I'll ensure they understand you're here for several weeks and that they'll have plenty of time to ask detailed questions later, when you're well rested. We'll be sure to get you back to the hotel early, so you can have a restful evening."

"Thanks, Claude. I appreciate that." Kevina hung up the phone.

She undressed quickly, laid out a fresh set of clothes, and stepped into the bathroom. After the shower, she dressed in front of the full-length mirrors. She walked out to her phone and started to dial Nigel, but stopped, looked out of the window to the northern hills, and dismissed the idea of calling him. She knew he must have called her many times, but she'd blocked all calls from him.

She put the phone down, thought about the upcoming events of the day, and walked slowly down the stairs to the lobby to await Claude's arrival.

In the car with Claude, she stated, "Claude, I'm assuming everyone who'll be attending is security cleared."

"Absolutely. To the highest level. In fact, you can't even enter our software lab unless you're Cleared Top Secret."

She was in front of a very receptive and eager audience of about fifty experts. After a brief introduction to the subject of cyber-warfare and cyber-terrorism—which had been under discussion in aviation circles globally lately—she directed her focus to the topic at hand. At issue, she said, was the global accomplishment that the air traffic management system had truly become interconnected and interoperable as one global system in a way that had not been possible before. However, this had also raised serious concerns regarding the vulnerability of the global ATM system. She pointed out that cyber-warfare had now assumed increasingly greater significance in our interconnected world.

She took a sip of water and continued, "Now, let us get down to specifics. The one method that a cyber-terrorist would use is to sabotage the ATM system from within. In some ways, this would be a digital microsimulation of the event that took place in the United States in New York on that fateful September morning, referred to as 9/11, at the turn of this century. The attack was from within the system. It is interesting to note that this was one scenario that planners of the national security systems of the day had not considered. The planners were not able to descend deep enough into the twisted minds of the terrorists to be able to fully understand their relatively simple plan, which we all know was very effective. The would-be terrorists had trained themselves to commit their horrible act in full view of the authorities. In the case we're considering, the overarching principle is very similar; only the sophistication is different. The lesson we all learned through that horrid event must be applied in aviation safety.

"Carefully consider this scenario: you have a legitimate flight progressing normally within the global air traffic management system. The flight management system in the aircraft originates what looks like normal, innocuous messages, but encoded in these messages are a bunch of carefully placed, hard-to-detect special characters that cause a momentary system interrupt, long enough to allow the entry of a special, self-replicating virus. Once in the system, the virus causes a serious enough malfunction to force a shutdown of air traffic management computer systems. The self-replicating virus grows and worms its way from one ATM system to another, across international and continental boundaries, and within less than thirty minutes, the global system—or a major portion of it—is impaired.

"Some of you may recall another significant cyber-event occurring at the dawn of this century. Some experts envisioned a meltdown of our computer systems worldwide in a scenario known then as the Year 2000—or Y2K—problem. Whether these computers were deployed in financial systems or ATM systems, the meltdown would have occurred as the world said goodbye to one century and welcomed the following one. Luckily for the world, concerted global action prevented the Y2K meltdown from occurring.

"But this time, with the scenario I just outlined, the attack from within would occur unexpectedly and deliberately by a highly trained, educated, demented, destructive mind. And there's more. The ATM system in many countries, including Iran, is connected with the defense system. So what might happen is that the virus could worm its way into the defense systems, thus jeopardizing general security.

"Let's play out this scenario a bit more. The knowledge that the security of Global Alliance countries is in jeopardy could be very useful to international terrorist groups. These forces of darkness who want to destroy our civilization will suddenly have the opportunity to stage multiple attacks in many forms against us. The relative peace that has prevailed over our world in recent years would be shattered, thrusting us all back into the Dark Ages from which we have only lately emerged."

She paused to survey the audience, which had been listening to her in pin-drop silence. A hand went up. She had said she'd entertain questions at any time, though she preferred questions at the end, simply because as a good presenter, she always tried to anticipate questions and provide answers before they were posed.

"Yes, sir. You have a question?"

"Dr. Paul, can you say something about this self-replicating software routine? Why would the normal data checking and security features not detect it and reject it?"

"Our current anti-virus software and shields should detect and reject most viruses trying to infiltrate our systems from external sources, but in the scenario I've outlined, the cyber-threat is being posed from an internal and apparently legitimate source. I submit to you that our system's anti-virus function is not as robust internally as it is against external interference and attacks. We need to increase our vigilance and do our best to anticipate how a terrorist's mind may thing, and try to safeguard our systems against every possible threat—external, as well as internal. An ill-intentioned person who knows our system well, is determined, and has the capability, could develop and introduce a destructive virus, a Trojan horse, into the operational system and wreak havoc in our current system."

Claude then rose and concluded the meeting, reminding all that this was the first introductory meeting and that Kevina would be available for several weeks for detailed discussions.

That evening, Claude invited her for an early dinner at a restaurant in the north of Tehran, near the hotel. Kevina accepted and decided to walk there. It was a cool evening; a gentle breeze caressed the landscape, and the bushes swayed gently. During the dinner, Claude had an interesting proposition.

"Why don't we use a modified ATM system simulator? Such a simulator, which would replicate the functionality of an operational ATM system, would serve as the test bed in which we can insert likely software viruses and cyber-attack scenarios to study the system's reaction. That way we can develop and test preventive measures and solutions."

Kevina was impressed at Claude's clear thinking, and she told him that it was exactly what was necessary. The simulator could be used to generate threat scenarios, and the system could be tested to see how it would withstand the simulated threats. Claude was confident that an up-to-date ATM simulator could easily be loaned to the project from the aviation training academy, which had many aircraft and ATM simulators for training both pilots and air traffic controllers.

Claude asked if she might take on the entire project, but Kevina said, "I don't wish to expand my role in order to manage the project on a hands-on, day-to-day basis, because that would require my full-time presence and dedication, from start to finish. I would, however, remain as the director-advisor of security and implementation consultant. One extremely important requirement is that all who work on this must have the highest security clearance. In fact, I insist all must have the ultra-highest security clearance, which is a level above top secret. Can we do that, Claude?"

"Sure. I'll ensure everyone here is at that level. I don't see any problem with the upgrades, which can be done very quickly. As far as you and the overall management of the project are concerned, we want you to have an advisory role, but with a difference: you must have executive veto power when you need it. We don't want any problem you raise to be buried in a report."

She agreed and felt satisfied. She had a short meeting with the VP of the Civil-Military Aviation Organization, Zakir Tandorost, who was genuinely pleased to meet her. He promised to meet her again very shortly, and with that, the meeting ended.

\* \* \*

Later, she met key project personnel, spoke briefly about the simulator, and asked the team to establish a brainstorming group. She reminded the software and systems engineering experts that they were to go well beyond what could be simulated and to think of all the weaknesses in the system. She spoke about where the focus of the engineering effort should be, on designing safeguards. Overall, she was pleased to that her team had on it some of the best software engineers in the world. The team had been recruited through General Software, a leading software engineering company, headquartered in Bengaluru, India. She had known of and worked with GS—one of the world's largest software houses—before.

GS's main achievement was that it had revolutionized the science of developing software. While others wrote papers on what could be and one day would be done, GS had developed specialized software for creating software. You told the system what capability you wanted in terms of required inputs, the processes to be applied, and the desired outputs, and the system spewed out the software within seconds. Under contracts with several automobile manufacturing companies in North America, Europe, and East and South Asia, GS had provided most of the software for self-drive automatic cars, generally referred to as e-Cars, and at times as smart cars.

Amazingly, while it was relatively easy to fully automate aircraft cockpits, the same could not be said for automobiles. The main reason was that aircraft generally operated in a fully definable and quantifiable environment, where the unknowns were extremely few. Of course, there was still the need for human pilots in passenger-carrying civil aircraft. No aviation authority in the world was even contemplating eliminating the human pilot, mainly because if an unusual situation ever arose, or the aircraft experienced a malfunction, trained human intervention would be instantly available. The pilot's role had become that of simply monitoring the performance of the aircraft, though in rare circumstances, he would be ready and able to take over by easily disabling the auto mode and manually guiding the aircraft to safety.

By contrast, the environment within which automobiles operated was not totally definable. There were countless scenarios for unanticipated conditions to arise on the roads. To have an automated capability within the automobile to address all such occurrences had proven difficult.

Many had predicted gloom and doom for software developers, as machines would eventually replace them, even in creative thinking, but, amazingly, after a brief period, the opposite had happened. Listening, seeing, talking, thinking machines had proliferated. Technology was beginning to bring freedom, hitherto unimagined: bank ATM machines recognized you and addressed you by name; and at airports and border crossings across North America, there was nothing more welcoming, Kevina knew, than to be greeted by an immigration officer at a border checkpoint even before you could present your electronic passport. It seemed all worth it. She knew the day was near when even the passports and credit cards would disappear. She was also aware that super-high technology was a double-edged sword, as it could prove lethal in criminal hands.

Little did she know these very thoughts would come to haunt her.

"Kay, you'll be working with someone you already know, I believe—Surin Dev will be our chief engineer and team leader. You'll act as his advisor," Claude said. "Surin's well known as a smart software and systems engineer and team builder. He's well liked here and looks forward to seeing you and working with you."

Kevina had known Surin for several years. She remembered the first time she'd met him at the University of Ontario, where she was a part-time lecturer in software engineering. Surin had been completing his masters in systems engineering. She'd come to know Surin and had developed a fondness for him over the course of several years, and she'd continued her professional association when he'd joined her company and worked there for a while. Surin also enjoyed a reputation as a person of high standards in ethics and probity.

Kevina's respect for Claude received another boost. She was impressed that he'd acquired her services and those of Surin Dev in such a short time.

"Yes, Claude, congratulations to you. Surin's truly a great professional and the right person for the challenge ahead. I'd be pleased to work with him. I look forward to meeting him."

Surin had been born in Durban, South Africa, sometime toward the end of the previous century. She knew that growing up he'd survived an environment of poverty and political and social upheaval to complete his education, mostly through scholarships in England and Canada. Surin had worked in her company for a while, quickly floating to the top as the chief engineer, buoyed by his sharp intellect, ever-flowing eloquence, and pleasing personality. As he scaled the corporate ladder, he had stepped on people who were, as he said, in the way of progress—he did not mean his personal progress. Over the years, Surin and Kevina had formed a good professional team in which she was the developer of concepts from a macro-sense, and he was the one who'd articulate those concepts into the language of mathematics and computers and manage his team for their implementation as user software.

Later, as he gained international recognition, the inevitable occurred: he was recruited by the world's leading software company, General Software, but continued to work in the defense and aviation fields. Their association continued, albeit from a distance.

She wrapped up the gathering by saying, "Remember that the current data-checking measures in the global ATM system are fairly rudimentary. Some of us, I know, have worked in military command and control systems where information warfare is well understood, and there are some very sophisticated measures in place. That expertise will be of great help. Please remember that the ATM interfaces with military surveillance systems of many countries in the world. What you will be doing is very important for both the military systems and the ATM, whose protection is, of course, our primary objective. I wish you all luck."

Back at the hotel, after her second quick shower of the day, overcome by a tiredness familiar to globe-trotters, Kevy simply crashed, disconnecting from the world. Deep into the night, her mind was uneasy. She saw herself over and over, looking very wooden. She dreamed she was surrounded by robots, but she could not tell herself apart from the robots. She woke up at the sound of the alarm and did her early meditation routine from bed.

That day, she met with Surin. Both were pleased to renew their association. Over the next few weeks, she completely immersed herself in the project. Most of her days were spent with the people on her team, giving them advice.

During her time at the office, she and Surin initially spent all their time planning the various stages of software development, and of course, the appropriate documentation, the key element that could not be neglected. Initially, both had to stipulate the software development and quality standards for all to follow. A crucial aspect of the whole project were the weekly, peer-level and management reviews. An independent testing and certification team also had to be set up.

She learned that Surin had been assigned from GS to the project. He was a specialist in military surveillance systems and had been the architect of several such systems for friendly nations in Europe and Asia. She became increasingly impressed with his abilities in general, and his technical depth in particular. He was also a mathematician and helped design many of the complex algorithms needed for data encryption. People working for Surin converted these algorithms into computer software programs. Over time, she realized how the entire project depended on this one man, how he was the one to hold the entire team together. He seemed to be everywhere and involved in all issues. Kevina had been in the software development business, and she knew that this was not an unusual situation.

True to her nature, Kevina was strictly business in the office, but toward the end of the longer days, she would occasionally indulge in small talk with him. One evening in the office cafeteria over a working dinner, she said to Surin, "Tell me more about your life growing up in Bengaluru."

That was when Surin had told her about his childhood and early life in South Africa. At the end of his narrative, he hesitated a bit before saying, "Tell me about yourself and your hubby. I think I met him briefly, years back."

"It's too complex a relationship to explain," she said, standing up and picking up her plate.

From her stance, he knew she didn't want to talk any further about herself. He got the clear message that it was simply prudent to let the matter of her private life hang in the air. In time, it would, perhaps, unfold.

He continued, "So, Kay, since I saw you last, I've moved around a bit, but mostly with GS, and I'm really enjoying it, as again and again, I get to meet very interesting people—like you."

She smiled but avoided his eyes, dumped the paper plate in the garbage can, picked up her coffee, and hurried out of the cafeteria to her office.

Over the next few days, Kevina talked to Surin quite a bit, but always about the project, avoiding any small talk with him. Surin responded in kind and maintained a professional but distant air. Her reliance on him, for the success of the project, grew to the point where it was total. Surin was pleased to note she'd placed considerable trust in him.

The project progressed.

Kevina spent a lot of time on her own. She

went for long walks in Tehran, in the woods not too far from the hotel. There was an inviting tranquility in the woods, a few evening strollers, bikers, and some hawkers selling Iranian teas and snacks.

Over time, she looked forward to these lone walks, and she began to enjoy her solitude. It was in this solitude that Kevina was able to look deeper into herself. During her brisk walk, she would detach herself from her physical being. She knew that it was very relaxing and refreshing to look at the greenery in the park. It was supposed to improve one's intellect and memory, as well.

Long ago, she had read *Walden* by Henry David Thoreau, who had explored the power and bliss of solitude. Thoreau had written of a "certain doubleness" by which he could "stand as remote" from himself as from another human. Thoreau had found solitude "companionable." During her walks, she finally understood Thoreau, who lived a long time alone in the Walden woods in what he described as a little world all to himself in which he "enjoyed the friendship of the seasons." The solitude gave him the opportunity to know himself better; the sentiment resonated with Kevina. Solitude was a time to know oneself. Like Thoreau, she never felt lonesome, or as he put it, "In the least oppressed by a sense of solitude." His solitude was almost total and everlasting, time spent with himself and no one else, while hers was only a few hours each evening, but she looked forward to her walks and times in quietude, nevertheless. It was then that the creative juices flowed, and she was able to identify problems, mostly technical, as well as potential solutions.

During the walks, she also thought about

her role in Iran, and though she and her team were there to make a meaningful and lasting contribution by making the international aviation system more secure, she felt a sense of disappointment, as well. She and the key players on her team could have easily been tasked to enhance the system with more features and capabilities, which is what likely would have happened just a few decades before. Now, in keeping up with the issues of the times, protection of national and international assets against every form of terrorism was equally important.

What was it that drove a person or a group to embark upon a path of destruction? Who were these people who took such pride in committing such acts only to claim responsibility for them with great chest-thumping pride? She concluded that no society on earth is or would ever be free of crime, and the world would always live under the threat of terrorism—a Damoclean sword hanging over the entire planet, and indeed, over modern civilization and the progress of the world. Perhaps this was the third world war. Unlike previous world wars, this would be a world war in perpetuity, with no likely end. Just as the world would never be free of criminal actions by humans—theft, embezzlement, murder, and so on—it seemed to her that the world would never be free of terrorism.

She often thought about Nigel and wondered what he was doing on her walks. Deep down, she actually missed him, though her resolve to wait for him to take the initiative remained unshakeable. Yes, she definitely needed the green light from him, and he had the means to do it quite easily.

The project also occupied her mind as she

walked, and she'd often analyze whatever discussions she'd had with her colleagues that day. Lately, she'd noticed that Surin seemed somewhat disturbed at times, looking increasingly tired. She thought she should ask but simply could not. She was aware he had a fairly tough responsibility, assigning, coordinating, and integrating the work of prima donnas who liked to work as a team, but had an individualistic air of independence. He was driven by the milestones in the schedule, and he went the extra mile to meet the deadlines. Of course, his compensation, along with that of many of his senior team members, depended on incentives designed by the company for those who'd met or exceeded the expectations.

One day, as she was about to turn in for the day and before turning out the lights, she took a last look at her computer screen and noticed there was a message for her. The message appeared on the screen:

*Dear Kevy,*

*You have awakened me to myself and what I had become, but now I am ready to change. I want to fill your life with a happiness and contentment you have not seen with me so far. For that, I am prepared to do anything to make you reconsider your decision and come back home.*

*Give me a chance.*

*Forever yours,*

*Nigel*

He was capable of tenderness, she had known, but she felt teary as she read and reread his brief message, conveying the right sense of urgency and tenderness she for which she had been hoping. She was quite pleased but decided to sleep on it.

# 6

Back in Toronto, after a night's restless sleep, Nigel got out of bed and decided to do something he hadn't done for a long while—he packed a couple of bananas and a water bottle and set out for the walking trail in the park about ten minutes from his house. As usual for a weekday morning, there was hardly anyone about, and Nigel was grateful for the solitude. He walked for an hour or so, amid the wood on either side of the winding trail, even though it was a bit uphill.

Long ago, Kevina had said to him, "Walk, Nigel. Walk as much as you can each day. A good walk refreshes the brain and opens it to inspiring thoughts." He understood the words, but not the message. He did not walk, certainly not in the park, but now that he had, he relished the new experience. Though he'd been alone during Kevina's travels, he never really discovered the true meaning of solitude.

The evergreens towered above him, casting their shadows consolingly over him and the trail. The temperature on that bright, late-spring morning was around fifteen degrees—almost perfect for a long walk. He saw a bench and sat down, his legs relieved. He unzipped his backpack and quenched his thirst from the water bottle. Now he felt different. She was right: he did find it rejuvenating to walk. He'd also reached the decision that instead of brooding, he'd look forward with positivity and find a solution.

What was it about human nature, he wondered, that made love between two people grow in the periods when the physical distance between them increased. How had he not seen the pain in her when he was readily capable of recognizing and feeling the pain of strangers? Tears welled up so easily in his eyes when watching human suffering, even in fictional movies, but he was insensitive to the internal suffering of the person sitting right next to him.

Someone once said that familiarity breeds contempt. Though Nigel was sure he had no contempt for Kevy, he wondered if the constant nearness and proximity between them had created a familiarity in which she was taken for granted and her true worth had diminished in his eyes.

"No, Nigel," he said to himself. "Look forward and find a solution, as there's no point trying to dig into why what happened happened." The onus for saving and invigorating the relationship, Nigel realized, was totally on his shoulders. He had to do something significant and positive, immediately. And he knew he would do it later that day.

He was satisfied at the clarity of this new direction that seemed to have dawned upon him from within himself. He wasn't sure if he was capable of the thoughts, let alone the action, that lay before him, but he knew he must move ahead decisively, and immediately so. He felt energized and ready to take action.

Nigel opened his shoulder bag, took out a banana and another water bottle, consumed them, and walked back. The walk back was easier; it was a gentle downward slope, almost all the way. At home, he immediately flipped open the kitchen computer. How many times had Kevy explained to him their finances and he'd done nothing save grunt his way through her tutorials? The program seemed to have anticipated his questions. A few graphs and tables depicted his financial position within seconds. He saw Kevy's hand in it and almost smiled at the ease with which he understood his financial state.

The next morning, he took a large box to the office, packed his personal belongings, and handed a letter to his boss.

*Dear Adam,*

*I've decided to take the offer of early retirement which was made to me in the company letter (attached). I actually have more than thirty days of leave owed me by the company. Therefore, as permitted by the company rules of retirement, I hereby give you the thirty-day formal notice of my retirement. You can let me know the effective date, as my last working day was a week ago, when I departed on leave. My family circumstances compel me to take this unexpected step, and I deeply regret any inconvenience, but I do believe the immediate impact of my departure won't adversely affect our normal operations.*

*I must say that I have greatly enjoyed working for the company and will be leaving with very good memories. I would have liked to offer my services, if required, as a consultant but feel that I will not be able to do this for the next six months, or so. After that time, I will contact you to see if any opportunities exist.*

*My points of contact remain unaltered, and you also have my bank address, and so on, so I will assume that you will complete the necessary transactions as required.*

*Finally, Adam, it has been a privilege knowing you all these years.*

*Regards,*

*Nigel*

Kevina was awakened from deep sleep by the harsh ringing of the telephone. She had forgotten to activate the do-not-disturb feature the night before. She answered the phone with an annoyed, "Yes?"

"Dr. Kevina Paul? I am extremely sorry to disturb you at this hour, ma'am, but this is Dave Summers from the Joint Intelligence Agency, the JIA. We have some important information."

"Uh...who is this? Do I know you?" she asked, but she did remember the Joint Intelligence Agency. Formerly the CIA, the JIA was now a joint agency run from Ottawa, with the United States, Canada, and NATO nations as the core members of the Global Alliance. Recently, several countries in Asia had also become members. Its prime raison d'être was to share counter-terrorism intelligence.

"No, ma'am, you do not know me, and I have never met you, but I know almost everything about you, down to the dates of birth of your father and all of your loved ones. We know you arrived only two months ago, but I now have some very important news for you. I've just flashed my JIA security number to verify my identity. Are you listening to me, ma'am?"

She saw the flash message, confirming the authenticity of the JIA caller, regained her composure almost completely, and said, "I've checked the security flash on my palmtop. Go ahead, please. I'm all ears." They began to communicate in JIA-secure mode so they could talk freely.

"Dr. Paul, there has been a serious coup attempt in Iran—we don't know exactly by whom—but it appears that President Zhiraghi has been overthrown and may no longer even be alive. As you may know, there have been a few splinter groups that have been around, and one of them has tried this caper. We don't expect widespread violence in the streets, but it would be in your best interest to stay on the hotel premises, close to your palmtop. At this time, there's no personal danger. The JIA office will be in touch with you with further instructions as necessary. Incidentally, the hotel phone lines are working intermittently. In any event, you have your palmtop. Keep it on and close to you at all times, and keep it in JIA security mode. I'll communicate with you only on that. Any questions?"

"Is there any secrecy surrounding this information?"

"No, not really. It'll be public knowledge within hours, anyway. We expect CNN to announce it any minute. One more thing: if the JIA decides to call you on your cell, please remember we'll flash a picture of an elephant on your phone screen first, and that'll be your new personal graphic code. Any messages coming to your cell without this picture should be considered unauthenticated and are therefore to be ignored. Please confirm that you understand."

"Yes, I do. Can I talk to Zakir Tandorost and my colleague Surin Dev about this? I think both of them are security cleared at the same level as me."

"Let me see...Yes, they are fully cleared, top-secret by JIA, and you can talk to them, but absolutely no one else, please. Understood?"

"Affirmative. No one else."

"Good night—or whatever is left of it." The phone went dead.

The clock showed five after five in the morning. There was no point in going back to sleep. Kevina got up and made herself a cup of herbal tea in her room to kill a few minutes. She figured that Tandorost was probably just be waking up. She picked up the phone and decided to call him, the one person she trusted the most in the country.

He picked up the phone on the second ring, answering with considerable alertness in his voice. "Hello, Tandorost speaking."

She knew the alertness in his voice betrayed his long experience within the aviation industry. Senior managers in aviation authorities the world over knew that the business of aviation never stopped and that emergencies could occur at any time. The ringing of a phone at home, even in the middle of the night, usually meant an operational problem and several hours without sleep.

"Zakir, this is Kevina."

"Yes, Kevina. I recognize your voice," he said. "It's only five-thirty. Something serious must be up, or you wouldn't be calling me at this early hour. What's up?"

"Zakir, I don't know if you're aware, but President Zhiraghi has been involved in some kind of political upheaval," she said, softening the actual news.

"Did you get this on CNN?"

"No, from a very reliable source: the JIA. You know them."

"Yes. So this can't be a hoax?"

"No, no chance of that, Zakir. I think it's very serious and fully authenticated from my side. At least you've been alerted."

"Okay, thanks. I do appreciate this heads-up. I'll be very busy for the next few hours, but I'll be in touch. I'll call your cell."

"Call me in secure mode only, please."

"Thanks, Kay." He hung up.

It was still very early in the morning. Out of her window, Kevy could see the city, ominous in the predawn darkness. She wondered what forces were at work trying to destabilize civilized society and what had motivated them to do so. For a while, she wondered whether she should call anyone, but decided against it. She activated her e-mail account—nothing unusual there. She then checked the company intranet and noted on the e-chat that some of the software people were at work, even at that early hour. From her long experience in software development, she knew it was not unusual to have software people working weird hours. Only highly motivated engineers would ever work on projects such as this. She looked for any names she recognized and was a bit surprised to find that Claude was at work, as well.

"Hey, Claude, shouldn't you be in bed?" she queried, using the chat feature.

"Surprise, surprise. I should ask you the same question," he replied.

"Well, I'm an insomniac."

"And in my case, I'm turning into one, what with this project and the tasks and deadlines you've imposed upon us."

"That's good. I like your dedication. Is Surin with you?"

"No. He'll be in a little later."

Surin was the Chief C3 Engineer from GS assigned to the project. She was a bit surprised he wasn't at work when the overall project manager was in. It quite unusual. She made a mental note to talk to Surin about it as soon as possible. Obviously, Claude wasn't aware of the political storm about to unleash itself on everyone. She knew not to say anything at this time, and she didn't.

"Look, Kevina, someone will pick you up at 8:00 a.m."

She was alert by then and had a quick comeback. "Claude, if you don't mind, I've had particularly bad night and I'm not feeling one hundred percent. Why don't I call you, and you can make arrangements to have me picked up then. Is that okay?"

"Certainly. You know how to reach me. Please, rest well. Take your time, because we can't afford to have you sick because you've overworked yourself."

Kevina disconnected with Claude and decided to give Surin a call. He answered, surprised to hear her voice, and said that he was in his car on his way to work. Kevina mentioned it was odd that Claude and his people seemed to be at work so early without him.

"Look, Kevina, I'll be passing by your hotel very shortly. Can I drop in, have a chat with you, and more importantly, show you some documents? It's important."

"Okay. The dining room on the ground floor will be open for breakfast, and I'll be down in twenty minutes waiting for you in a quiet corner. It shouldn't be too busy this early."

She quickly freshened up, went down to the dining room, and met Surin. They found a table in the corner and ordered tea. He appeared restless.

"Kevy," he said suddenly, "I've been trying to get your attention over the last few days to discuss an issue, but you've been acting so stand-offish. I wanted to express my apologies because I went too far delving into your personal life the other day. I only did it because I thought we were fairly good friends."

"That we will always be. Now, what's the issue?" She zeroed in on the subject at hand, deferring personal chit-chat to a later time, deciding to hear his side before revealing the news of the impending political upheaval.

"Well, Kay, there are things going on that I'm not aware of. It seems Claude has some kind of parallel effort going on. Now, I know Claude's involved in several projects, and it's not unusual for him to multi-tasking, but what I've noticed is that our top-secret software is being copied and taken to another location. I've already made arrangements for contingency planning in case of a disaster at the centre, so it's not for that—that's one of the first things I do, and everyone on the project is aware of the disaster recovery plan.

"You know, I feel like I'm being used for a surreptitious objective. I also feel some of the lead software developers have tasks other than the ones I've imposed on them. I'm worried; it's not in his interest to hide things from me.

"This is a massive project. We have teams in Toronto, San Francisco, and Bengaluru all working to develop separate packages to be integrated here, in Tehran. There were no specific modules assigned to any team here, because as you know—and as Claude knows—integration is the most difficult and time-consuming job. We have our hands full, already. What other work is he doing with our software that I don't know about?

"Kay, I fear there may be a really big blow up this afternoon between him and me. I've called a meeting with him, and I'm going for his jugular. Several governments have been spending big money and time on this—I see a screw-up coming, and I'm not going to allow it."

Kevina knew him well enough to let him finish—once Surin started to talk it was difficult to stop him. He was also uncharacteristically agitated. She got the picture. The most disturbing aspect was that some software was being moved out of the secure facility, and neither Surin nor she knew exactly why.

"I smell something bad, but I don't know if there's a rat," he concluded. "I've obtained and printed out this software documentation without anyone's knowledge—take a look at this."

Surin's suspicions reminded Kevina of her own lack of trust in Claude. However, she thought the time wasn't right to add her own prejudice over

Surin's concern.

Kevy asked, "Can I keep this documentation till we meet this evening?"

"Yes, of course. Please go over the docs. Let me know if you see the same demon I do."

"Now, before I tell you something very important, I want to ask you if you saw anything unusual in the streets at all."

"No. Everything was quiet; the city's just waking up. Why?"

"Well, I just got a top-secret call from the JIA. There's been a coup attempt. Details are sketchy, but the president is missing. People in the street don't seem to be aware, but that'll change as soon as the international media are aware. I just alerted Zakir to it. Right now, the JIA doesn't know who the perpetrators of the coup are. We have to be careful—this is all secret, of course, and cannot be revealed to Claude, or anyone. Maybe you'd rather stay at the hotel instead of going to the office. What do you think?" She looked up at the Dubai News on the TV on the wall, but there seemed to be no mention of Iran.

"Wow, Kay. A coup. It's a bit surprising because politically, everything's looked very good here. There's stability and economic progress in the country. I thought the president was well-liked. Anyway, I have to go and meet Claude, since I was the one to set up the meeting. My not turning up will arouse suspicion, for sure.

"I'll be careful, and if I see any problem at all, I'll return right here and be in touch with you."

He stood up to leave. Kevina counselled him to pose the questions to Claude in a cool and professional manner, and they made arrangements to get together that evening. He agreed not to mention their meeting to anyone.

"Meanwhile, take care. Pretend you don't know anything. Send me a text when you're safe at the office."

He waved goodbye. Kevy remained sitting, looking out of the huge doorway into the lobby.

Outside, the city was greeting the dawn of a new day in its normal fashion, the human and vehicular traffic building up to its daily peak. She tried to analyze what Surin had said. Was there any link between what Surin had revealed and the looming political upheaval? The coincidence was both noteworthy and troubling at once. She took the documentation up to her room, put the Do Not Disturb notice on the doorknob, and started going through the documents in a methodical manner.

She switched the TV on to catch any development about the coup in any of the news channels, though so far, there was nothing. Even CNN seemed not to be in the know.

Nigel heard the engines roar. The aircraft gathered momentum, and at the end of its run, leaped into the air, and commenced the noise abatement procedure prescribed for all aircraft departing Toronto. He was on a flight bound for Dubai. Nigel had spent considerable time trying to think like Kevina. A realization dawned on him that he loved her so much he had to find her. While he couldn't change the past, he knew the future would be different—very different. He was taking the first step to implementing his plan to win her back, and he was satisfied.

Nigel tried hard to recall the recent projects in which she had been involved and remembered Kevy mentioning the Middle East several times. Even when she was weary of business travel, there was always a twinge of excitement, however muted, whenever she went to that region of the world. She spoke very fondly of the remarkable people she'd met there and the progress the countries were making toward democratic governments. He finally concluded the Middle East was the most likely place for her to go.

Dubai was easy to fly to and operate from, but there was another, much more important reason for that: Jim Periwinkle, a reliable friend and Brit businessman who had lived for a long time in several countries in the Middle East. Over the years, Jim had built up a wide network of contacts in the region, with branches or affiliate companies in several countries in the Middle East.

A few days before leaving, Nigel had called him. Kevy had met Jim almost fifteen years earlier, and over the years, Nigel had also had gotten to know Jim quite well, as he'd visited them in Toronto several times, as they had him, in Dubai. Jim—as Kevy had mentioned and he had observed several times—was a fairly important part of the British presence in Persian Gulf countries.

It was amazing how the Brits ran large business establishments, advised governments, and still managed to have a great time. The major hotels, the clubs, and the entertainment industry in general, catered to them. The days of the British Empire were long gone, but the Brits, to their credit, had managed to retain all the advantages of the empire and dispose of the burdens. He thought of the Ocean Breeze Golf Club in Dubai, which represented the best of British culture and was a reminder of the good old, supposedly bygone, days of British dominance in Asia, complete with

English brews and uniformed waiters, mostly from the subcontinent.

In the region, Jim operated as a wheeler-dealer, a businessman par excellence. The main reason Nigel was anxious to meet with him was because he'd either know Kevy's whereabouts or be able to find them out, there was no doubt about that. A few years earlier, Kevy and Nigel had helped Jim when his wife of more than thirty years had been diagnosed an alcoholic. That relationship narrowly escaped divorce, but was back on track after Zoe, Jim's wife, had enrolled in a treatment program.

Upon his arrival at the Dubai airport, Jim and Zoe were already waiting for him. Jim gave him a warm handshake, and Zoe hugged him.

"We're so glad to see you, Nigel, but I felt it was a little too sudden, so what's up, and how is Kevy?" Over the next few hours, Nigel slowly unrolled the events in a frank and open manner. Jim and Zoe asked few questions but grasped the situation. Jim made a few calls and felt that, with his contact with aviation authorities in the region, he should be able to find her whereabouts within a few days.

"Nigel, we want you to stay here with us while you're here. We have a guest suite. You and Kevy stayed there before. You know you can have your privacy when needed, but you're still with us and can have all of your meals with us if you choose. So relax, and try polishing up your golf and tennis games. Meanwhile, I'll be doing all I can to locate her and keep you informed in real time. How does that sound?"

Nigel accepted the offer gratefully.

Over the next few days, Nigel got up very

early and either played a round of golf with Jim or tennis with Zoe. Even though both kicked his butt handily, he enjoyed the sessions nevertheless. On those outings, he thought a lot about Shelly, and in the quietness of those mornings, he'd also feel her presence. He knew Shelly would have wanted him to find Kevy.

It was a long time ago, but Nigel and Kevina had met first on the tennis courts in Richmond Hill, north of Toronto. The club pro had paired them randomly as a mixed-doubles team. They had clicked and later went on to win the club championship. Kevina was also a very good singles player and was the champion or runner-up several times over. Later, he'd taken her out for dinner, and the more he came to know her, the more amazed he became of her. He'd once asked her, "Kevina, is there a limit to your abilities? When and where will you stop and say, 'This is it; I don't want to do anything more'?" A few months later, he thought his heart might explode with joy when she told him one evening, "Nigel, I'm not sure when and where my journey will stop, but I think I've stopped searching for a life partner."

They were married six months later.

One evening, Jim called Nigel and said, "We've checked all the likely countries in the region except for Iran. Curious thing—just as we were checking up with our contacts there, I was informed there was a coup attempt. Right now, all communication with Iran seems to be suspended. Nigel, I'm doing my best, but right now, looking for Kevy in Iran is like looking for a needle in a haystack on fire. I'm keeping a close eye on the situation and have some very good in-country contacts.

"You have to be patient, Nigel. Waiting can be very tough. It'll be particularly hard for you. Play golf and tennis—we'll get you a two-month guest membership at the Dubai Tennis and Cricket Club. Zoe and I can play with you in the evenings, work, my knees, and her bridge games permitting. I know, at one time, you were very good. Look at this as an opportunity, Nigel. Instead of going crazy waiting for me to find the whereabouts of your wife, you can see how you can work on this roll of flab here." Jim poked him in his side and laughed. "In fact, there aren't too many other options."

Nigel understood the situation, but he felt concerned for Kevy's safety, nevertheless. He resolved not to let himself drown in a worry-well until he knew where she actually was. He had a lot of faith in Jim's reach through his network of contacts; Kevy had mentioned several stories associated with Jim's influence in the region.

As a legitimate registered company representative or local agent, Jim had represented some of the top American, British, and Canadian companies in the energy, mining, and aerospace sectors. He was well connected, and he brought good results for his clients. The other great quality of his, very much appreciated by his clients, was that he had never been in any trouble, having steered clear of any shady or suspect deals. There was a level of comfort with him. He did favors for a lot of prominent people, banking them in a mental database until he was able to collect a favour in return, be it in business, or for personal reasons.

# 7

On the TV back in her room, news of the Iranian coup attempt had finally broken out. President Zhiraghi was under detention, his exact whereabouts unknown, and there was no statement from him. The Iranian Defense Forces appeared to be in a state of disarray. The IDF commander in chief had assured the public on TV that the IDF was solidly behind the president, and was doing everything it could to ensure his safety and catch the perpetrators, but would not provide any details. Kevina had always felt the IDF senior officers she'd met seemed to be pro-Zhiraghi. However, there were reports in the media that some men in uniform were seen in the streets, and they seemed to be supportive of the coup. She was also aware that Iranian politics were quite inscrutable. Not a single political pundit had sounded even a dim, distant warning of the upheaval. Of course, now, analysts would be coming out of the woodwork with elaborate explanations as to what had precipitated the recent events and what would happen in the immediate future.

The announcement of a caller from the lobby

shattered Kevy's train of thought.

It was Surin. "Doc, you and I need to talk," he said.

She met him in the lobby bar minutes later where, over hot tea and non-fat, no-sugar cookies, Surin narrated his findings. He told her that Claude had changed the entire action plan.

"They're spending all their time building a system that could be used to generate messages containing destructive viruses to disrupt the air traffic management system. It started off as a simulator, but some selected key workers have been assigned full-time to the simulator project while the few remaining are working on the security system. There's been no consultation with me at all, and many of the project's progress reviews, which we'd all attended, were actually fake. Claude's personally directing the simulator effort. He's been using me to help make the simulator more and more robust. Claude has people working round the clock on shifts in order to complete the simulator project to meet a deadline that's been imposed on him by someone, or so it seems. Kay, there's a project within a project. Their real project's wrapped up in a fake shell. What do you think could be going on?"

"Let us think: first, do you have access to the software programs library where the programs are being deposited after their development?"

"Yes, I do. I've designed and organized the entire setup. The entire software library's been copied onto a high-density, USB drive in my briefcase. So, Doc, we can determine exactly what they're up to. I have my laptop with me—we can examine the software."

Kevina said, "Great. We can start immediately, then, but we'll need privacy. We'll also have to be very careful to ensure no one suspects anything. Let's go to my suite where I can use my computer as well."

For the next ten hours, they used their combined expertise to analyze what Claude was really up to. Modern software is written in something akin to plain English language. It's easy to read through and understand, especially when done by two knowledgeable people. After several hours, Kevy came to the conclusion that what she had in front of her was the software for a simulator that would generate malicious software, a destructive virus, which—if transferred to an aircraft electronic flight management system—would worm its way into the regional air traffic management system and disrupt regional air traffic flow with huge implications for the safety of life and property. The interesting feature of the malicious software was that it could be easily hidden in normal operational messages from the cockpit to the ATC centre's ATM software. They were cleverly constructed so as to pass through the ATM system's normal security software.

Her concern was further heightened when she realized the virus had the capability to self-replicate. This meant that the virus was able to spawn multiple copies of itself to wreak havoc across the globe, which was very frightening. Who would think of such a thing besides the well-trained, sophisticated mind of a terrorist? The scenario she'd tried to warn everyone about was beginning to take shape right under her nose—with her help, in fact.

"Kay, what do you think's going on? Everything I've seen over the last little while is meant for a virus generator."

"That is true, Surin. I've yet to see one line of code that has anything to do with system protection. It seems someone's writing a system destructor, rather than a protector."

"They've used all my mathematical routines but applied them in a very sophisticated virus. Their genius is that they've actually figured out exactly how to launch this monstrous mother virus."

Hour by hour, they decoded the computer language to give body and substance to the dastardly scheme hatched by Claude and his cronies. Before long, a very disturbing picture had begun to emerge.

"It is amazing. He's used me, and he's used you, and we didn't even know it. Kay, he's used us to help design a virus to destroy the world of aviation."

"You know, Surin, I know exactly how they're going to get the virus into the ATC computers: they'll do it from within the system. What I mean is that they could easily load it up along with a new flight plan in the aircraft's flight management system."

Kevina continued, "Then, they could fly the aircraft on a normal flight and let the aircraft FMS send the message—posing as a routine aircraft position report, weather report, aircraft flight intention change report, or anything seemingly normal. The two questions now are: how do we confirm our findings, and to whom do we report our findings. This is a real problem for both of us, Surin. We're both under contract with Claude, and he's up to no good. Let's think this through and determine exactly what steps we need to take."

They lapsed into prolonged silence. Kevina tore her eyes away from the screen and looked out the window—sometimes it helped to focus on something distant, an unrelated object, to clear the cobwebs from the mind. She took several deep breaths and tried to think clearly. She looked toward Surin who was stretched out on the sofa and away from the computer screen, his eyes closed.

The enormity of what she'd helped unearth fully dawned upon her. She, the one who had been trying hard to warn the aviation world of a near-doomsday scenario, had helped to create the very thing she'd warned against. She recalled reading about Einstein's despondency when he'd realized his famous equation has been used in the creation of the deadliest weapon of mass destruction, the atomic bomb, setting off one of the most horrifying arms races between Germany and the United States and the UK. She then recalled the plot the Allies had hatched to sabotage the heavy water plant in Norway, crucial to setting off a chain reaction in the atomic bomb.

She looked at Surin, still on the sofa, and said, "Surin, I have a few thoughts."

"Let's hear them, Doc. I have a few ideas to share as well."

"The one man I trust is Tandorost, so I need to talk to him. I also need to ask for advice from the JIA regional office. What do you think?"

"Doc, if I talk to my HQ in Bengaluru they'll want to pull me out of here on the next flight, then they'll go after Claude through legal channels. I feel, given where we are and what we've unearthed, we have a responsibility to see if there's anything we can do to sabotage Claude's evil scheme. Right now, you and I are the only ones in the world who are fully in the know and in a position to do something to avert a major disaster."

Surin continued, "One idea that's come to mind—see what you think—is that I take their virus, now that I understand it, and change it enough to destroy their virus and virus generator forever, putting an end to their efforts. It'll be like a Trojan horse within a Trojan horse. I think that while you talk to the people you have to, I'll set a time bomb for them that'll kick in as soon as they try to download the malware into an aircraft flight management system or link it with the FMS in any way. This way, nothing will happen till they try to load the simulator software into an operational FMS. Do you see what I'm getting at?"

"That's brilliant, Surin. Your virus killer is activated only if they try something they're not supposed to. It'll lie dormant in the system, quite harmless, until then. Later, at the right time, you can remove it, and no one need ever know about this whole affair. Right?"

"Precisely. I do need to get to the office for a few minutes, though, to make it appear as if everything's normal. The streets are safe, the police are everywhere, and there's no sign of any problems at all. If it's okay with you, I'll be back in less than an hour, and then I'll finish all the work here, in this lounge. Okay?"

"Go right ahead. Here's the electronic key—you need to enter the hotel and use it only once on the door to my suite. The door will remember your fingerprint and open automatically every time you touch the door."

Surin left. Kevy first called Dave Summers, the JIA operative who'd called her earlier, alerting her to the coup. Her phone had captured his phone number when he'd called. She connected with him in secure mode.

"Yes, Dr. Paul? What seems to be the problem?"

"Well, Mr. Summers, I'd like to consult with you to seek your advice on a situation that's arisen here." She summarized the situation in words that a non-expert would understand.

He listened in stony silence. "Go ahead, Dr. Paul."

"Please call me Kay. Everyone does."

"Okay, Kay. Then please call me Dave."

She then went on to tell him what had happened at her office in the software labs as well as Claude's suspicious activities. Dave seemed to be quite tech savvy and didn't have much difficulty grasping the overall situation.

He said, "I'm glad you told me this. It's good insight into what appears to be a very complex situation. Unfortunately, I can't tell you more, but this is very interesting—it fits right into the overall situation emerging. By the way, don't pay much attention to what you hear in the media. As usual, they don't know anything significant at all. There appears to be no real danger to you or to the general public in the streets."

"Outside life seems to be moving quite normally, though CNN did report there was a coup here."

"Yeah, we know."

"Is there anything I can do?"

"No. Make sure you guys don't mention this to anyone at all—this is very important. I'll confer with our aviation expert and may call you back if I need anything. Stay cool." The line went dead.

Kevina had been to JIA HQ several times, and she knew the duty officers at the intelligence centre were following countless bits of information, data, and tips and attempting to weave everything into cohesive situation reports.

She wondered if she'd be able to reach Zakir Tandorost. She decided to give it a shot, but she wouldn't initiate a discussion with him as to what Claude was up to. Zakir answered the phone. He was breathing very heavily, obviously tired and apprehensive. He seemed quite upset because, he explained, he was virtually under house arrest, apparently for his own protection, as the cabinet had ordered members of the top echelon of the government be given around-the-clock protection and to remain indoors for what appeared to be an indefinite amount of time.

"You know, Kevina, this kind of disruption is the last thing we need in this country. Also, the timing of this is particularly bad. We were poised to take significant steps forward in several areas of our economy, and we'd already made an impressive start and now this had to happen. I hope it blows over, but..."

His voice trailed off in a well of self-doubt. Kevina understood and tried to sound as optimistic as possible.

"Zakir, look at it this way: out in the streets, the military seems to be protecting its human assets, which means they still have the power. I'm sure this will soon be seen as a storm in a teacup, and the current government will be stronger for it."

"Yeah...Anyway, Kevina, right now, we're out of options. The entire airspace has been closed.

Only special and emergency flights are operating in our airspace. You be careful. I'll call you later."

That was the signal for Kevina to bid him goodbye, at least for the time being. She felt he knew more than he was saying, but he was under a gag order just as she was, and silence on both sides was the best course of action.

On the TV, specific information about what was going on was missing, but it wasn't stopping the media analysts from coming to their own conclusions as to the cause of the problem. They'd already attributed the blame to a shortfall in Western policies and inadequacies of the present regime in Iran. Analogies between the Zhiraghi regime and that of the shah's had been drawn. Kevina turned her mind off the TV.

She continued her review of the last bits of simulator software documentation, becoming even more convinced that she and Surin were on the right track.

She heard three knocks on the door. It opened, and Surin stepped in. He seemed calm and collected. He actually looked fresh, and she wondered if he'd had a shower at the office.

He opened his laptop, spread the documents on the dining room table, and plunged into the task at hand: developing the virus killer. Rather than calling the hotel restaurant or going to the restaurant for food, Kevina went downstairs to the grocery store in the hotel basement to pick up dinner for the two of them.

Nigel checked to see if there'd been an e-mail from Kevy.

*Nigel,*

*I'm safe. Don't worry about me. Will communicate with you.*

*Kevy*

Yes, this was Kevina to the core, no question about it—to the point and economical with words. No small talk, and above all, cautious. He saw a significant hidden message in those few words: she was safe, accessible from a communications standpoint, and responsive. Though she didn't hint at any reconciliation, her stance was definitely not negative. Her acknowledgment of his earlier e-mail and this short response was actually an indication that the door to their reconciliation had been left open. Now, if only he could determine where this message was coming from...

Regardless, he felt quite excited in the knowledge that she wasn't far and that he'd see her soon. Jim was also expecting a tip from his contact in Iran, sometime soon.

Of course, this coup in Iran had delayed their ability to get the information they needed, but Jim had a lot of ways and he knew a lot of people. Jim was awaiting a reply from his key contact in Tehran and told Nigel that he'd definitely get a call from the contact within a couple of days. Nigel had little choice but to continue to stay afloat in a sea of expectation and hope. He submerged himself in the social activities available, captivated by Jim and Zoe's hospitality and charm. Zoe kept assuring Nigel that Kevina and he would ultimately get back together.

Jim made multimillion-dollar deals in the

Gulf region. There were lots of tales on how he'd swung the deals. Nigel remembered that megadeal for the US Celerity fighter aircraft a few years earlier that he'd pulled through for a US-Canadian consortium in competition with a European consortium. The technology was very similar—both the aircraft had been fully evaluated by Gulf Defense Federation pilots and technicians, and the price was literally pennies apart, so what would break the tie? The decision was mired for months in the political dogfight that ensued as both sides tried to outdo the other with offers and counter-offers. The real issue, underneath all the posturing and stunts in the media, was which company would provide the sweetest deal for GDF. The manner in which companies sought to sweeten deals and enhance their positions was to offer socio-economic-industrial benefits, which could include local manufacturing and the establishment of related industries in the Gulf region, with the focus to create high-quality employment and diversification of the industrial base in the region. Promises of opening aerospace research facilities, the transfer of technology, and co-manufacturing were played out almost blow-by-blow in the media, while deals were cooked in private rooms, and whitewash strategies were hatched on golf courses.

Jim, it was said, was an influential player in the ultimate win by the US-led consortium. Of course, you could never get Jim to talk about the whole affair except in the most general terms. He got paid, presumably, very handsomely for his efforts.

Nigel knew that companies and consortia from the United States and other countries paid hefty commissions to their in-country agents.

Aware of the goings-on, Western governments, and a few non-profit organizations watched the international transaction closely, threatening prosecution for any wrong-doings. Many said Jim was above this, and so it appeared to Nigel and Kevina. In fact, Jim had too much at stake and too much to lose to dabble in illegal or unethical practices. Lately, Jim and Zoe had even been talking about retiring back to California.

Zoe played a good tennis game and great golf and talked a lot about life and love. Zoe reminded Nigel of a grown-up Shelly. Intuitive and sometimes stunningly insightful, she was a person able to get below the surface and find comfort there, though her opinions on the regional political situation were at odds with prevailing views.

She had said, several times, that beneath the seemingly apparent state of relative peace and calm in Asia, there was a subterranean layer, where the roots of extremism were somewhat stymied, but not dead. At times, she worried these negative forces might be growing. She'd been almost prescient in this regard, having witnessed the coup attempt in Iran. This was totally unforeseen and seemed to have happened just when foreign investments were pouring into Iran.

With respect to Nigel's predicament, she'd said with her well-known frankness, "Nigel, you've taken Kevina for granted. Kevy is everything a man could ever want—beautiful, very smart, accomplished, but modest, caring, and kind. You held a jewel in your hands and failed to recognize it. Face it, Nigel, it's the truth."

Nigel had always rejected the concept of unconditional love. His experience with life had taught him there was conditionality attached to all love. However, with the appearance of Shelly on his landscape, his view had been swept aside by his surging emotions for her. To his delight, Nigel discovered a beautiful side of himself that he had not been aware existed. He knew that he let it happen—love has to be demonstrated and nurtured, and in doing so, it grows. Nigel had forgotten this little lesson of life was a universal truth.

Nigel also recognized the stark and hurtful truth in Zoe's words. "Yes, Zoe, I know that now. Tell me something I don't know, like how do I fix this situation? How can I make up with Kevy, obliterate the past, and create the heaven I should have had and could have had but didn't?"

"Go find her, Nigel. Go to the ends of the earth, if you have to, but find her. When you meet her, look into her eyes and you will know what to say. Don't hold back. Make it up to her. Say it and mean it. It is simple as that, at least, from a woman's standpoint."

# 8

The challenge before Surin was to write an effective software virus, a Trojan horse, and that particular task was not a difficult one for him—hackers had been doing just that for decades. His challenge was to ensure the Trojan would lie dormant and untraceable, becoming self-invoked when an attempt was made to load the entire simulator software onto an aircraft. Then the Trojan would first corrupt and destroy the aircraft database—that repository within a computer system containing all the operational information. The normal aircraft computer program, when it found data that didn't make logical sense, would grind to a halt and set off a chain reaction until the entire aircraft became inoperative. Surin would have to find the appropriate hooks within the simulator so his program would lay dormant when the simulator was used in its intended mode.

He immersed himself in the task at hand. Shortly, Kevina returned with some sandwiches, a box of cereal, and a carton of milk from the hotel grocery store.

Surin looked up and said, "Kay, we need to

have a code name for our Trojan horse. Can you think of something that makes sense in some way?"

"Well, downstairs, while looking at our lunch options, I remembered that whenever the JIA and similar organizations embark upon such endeavors, they always come up with a name and I thought of Caviar Emptor, you know, after the special Iranian caviar from Caspian sea sturgeons. I recall reading that there was considerable concern over the aggressive fishing of sturgeons which nearly led to their extinction and there was once a movement called Caviar Emptor. We could even simplify it to Operation Caviar."

"Sounds good. Let's go with that. We can call it Caviar for short."

She commenced reviewing Surin's Trojan horse code, now Operation Caviar, as Surin continued completing the software.

Surin could not help wonder at how simplified the world of modern software development had become. The software development tools that thrust their creator, General Software—now his company—into prominence permitted developers to write sophisticated and complex software in plain language, almost within minutes. They had connected—the new term was "mated"—their laptops together and were exchanging data as she verified what he was writing, almost simultaneously with him writing it. Though both were aware of their physical proximity to each other, they continued unwaveringly, concentrating on their work, exchanging words only as they related to the task at hand. Surin thought she'd caught him looking at her a few times, and he felt a bit embarrassed, but then he had also caught her staring at him when his eyes were on his laptop.

They both knew time was of the essence. Whatever could be done had to be done quickly, especially because of the political upheaval that had hit the country.

After several hours and several cups of clear Iranian tea, they seemed to be at the end of their combined endeavour.

"What's next, Surin?" Kevina stood up, walked to the sofa, and stretched out.

Surin got up, stretched, sipped some tea, and stared out the open window, breathing in the outside air. It was a beautiful, early spring evening, which was yielding slowly but surely to the darkness of the night.

"I need to take the software and implement it on the system at the centre so it becomes a seamless part of Claude's package. Only then will what we've done so far mean anything. I need to do this alone and right now."

Kevina nodded in full agreement with him. At that stage, Surin could not take the risk of arousing suspicion. If they both appeared together at the end of the day, it was sure to raise some eyebrows. It was because of this she had to stay at the hotel and he alone would go to install the new software.

"But what if anyone challenges you?" she asked.

"I'll invite them to sit in with me and watch as I implement the software on the system. I know there's a list of minor bugs with the mathematical routines that need to be fixed, and really, I'm the one who's best suited to do the fixing, because most of them are my routines, and they all know it. The only problem that could arise if they suspect what we're up to here and decide to put together a team to analyze what we've done, line by line. They'd figure out our scheme in about three months," said Surin reassuringly.

Ready to depart, he packed up his laptop and walked to the door.

Kevina followed him. "Surin, please be careful. I'm a bit nervous."

Surin looked at her, a bit surprised at her expression of concern toward him, and saw that she'd stepped forward, extending her arms for a parting embrace. He slid into her arms, put his arms around her, and hugged her. She looked up at him and he returned her look as they continued to hold each other.

The embrace lingered. He kissed her lightly; she parted her lips. He locked his gaze with her and kissed her deeply, their tongues dancing a love tango that went on and on until she moaned with a deep longing. His hands massaged her back gently and slowly. His hand went inside her shirt and his fingers undid the clip on her bra. Meanwhile, with his other hand, he unbuckled the belt holding her skirt and her shirt, bra, and skirt slid onto the floor. He bent down a little, slid his arm around her knees, picked her up, and carried her to the bedroom.

A short while later, Surin slid out of the bed.

"Kevy, I wish I could just stay here, but I have to go. I'll keep you updated on the mobile using the secure mode."

He dressed, left the bedroom, and she heard his footsteps fade slowly away on the carpeted corridor. She got up and went to the window. A few minutes later, as she saw him get into his car and speed away, she heaved a sigh of relief.

Going down the elevator, the faint but combined aroma of her perfume and her body lingered. He relished the moments spent with her. How he wished it could have been extended, but the burden of the responsibility he'd assumed combined with his professionalism had crushed the desire to extend the moment. He knew the task ahead of him was awesome and strategically significant. He wondered if there'd ever be another time, if there'd be a future for them, or if this was simply a single episode and nothing more.

There were, however, other more important developing issues at that particular moment.

He knew that they'd have to plan his escape from Tehran fairly soon. Sooner or later, Claude and his gang would see the impact of what he had done, and then it would be a matter of time before they'd associate him with the sabotage of their devilish plans. When they did, he realized that both he and Kevina would be in danger. He resolved to ensure that his escape, whenever warranted, would include Kevina. He felt responsible for her safety alongside his own. They'd fly together to some safe and secure location that wouldn't arouse suspicion. So, what were the options? They'd need to think through a credible story.

Surin would have to address that later. Right now he had to ensure his full attention remained focused on the issue at hand. He stopped at his residence and walked over to his apartment. In the shower, he could think about nothing but Kevina's passion. He was aware of her current matrimonial predicament. He searched for a meaning and finally concluded it was simply a spontaneous gesture without a latent, long-term promise of any kind. Most likely, it was a dead end. He turned the shower off, dried off, stepped into a new set of clothes, hopped into his car, and drove off to the centre.

The biometric identity system at the centre recognized him. He flashed his card at the optical reader—a confirmatory gesture required by the slightly outmoded system. The doors opened to let him in. In his office, he cancelled the normal link to his e-mail and plunged right away into the task at hand.

    Within minutes of his arrival, he heard a knock on his office door. It was Claude. He wondered whether the sudden appearance of Claude within minutes of his arrival meant he was being watched, but Surin had his plan.

    Claude said, "Hi, Surin, I haven't seen you for—"

    Surin immediately cut him off. He knew he'd have to go into attack mode. "Claude, you know the problems we've been having with some of the routines—you must have seen some of the reports by the test managers. I've been working on fixes to the algorithms. I have the fixes now, and I want to implement them on the system. Could you have Latif and Alam join me so they know what's going on in case I'm not around?"

    "Oh, it's good you have the fixes. I was worried after I saw the problem reports. I'm afraid both Latif and Alam went home about an hour ago. They'd been working non-stop for over twelve hours—I had to practically push them through the door."

"Okay, Claude, why don't you sit with me?" This tactic of Surin's would hopefully accomplish two things. The first was to help remove any festering suspicion, and the second was to make sure that Claude stayed away from him for the next few hours. He knew that despite all his pretenses, Claude was not a software expert and always manage to wriggle out of the details.

After a few minutes of looking over Surin's shoulder, Claude walked away, and Surin smiled at how easy it was to get rid of him. He submerged himself in the task of concealing his Trojan horse in the vast and complex lines of code of the simulator. Several hours later, he'd satisfied himself that he'd accomplished what he'd set out to do. His cellular phone rang; it was in secure mode which was known only to one person who was currently in Iran.

Surin remembered that there was a history to what he was trying to achieve. It was sometime in the early 1980s when a pipeline management system had been stolen by Russians. What the thieves didn't know at the time was that a Trojan horse had been pre-planted in the system. Once they'd ported the software onto their own system and activated it, the entire system had been taken over by the Trojan horse and it exploded. The explosion was of such a magnitude that the fire was detected by international satellites.

What he was doing was similar, except there wouldn't be a visible explosion, simply a meltdown of the functions and capabilities of the simulator system. Only the people present at the time would be aware there was something wrong, and it might take them a long while to figure out the real cause of the system's catastrophic malfunction.

# 9

Kevina recovered slowly from her encounter with Surin, feeling quite weary and overcome with a deep sense of guilt. What was she searching for in life? Perhaps life was all about searching, as both a means and an end in itself. There was no destination in life but a continuing search. And it was not a search for anything in particular, certainly not for anything material.

She sighed, a torrent of conflicting thoughts continued in her mind. She remembered Nigel's e-mail. She had to come to a decision on the way forward in her personal life. There was no alternative for her to dismiss what had just happened with Surin as a spur-of-the-moment occurrence, where her normal sense of caution had yielded to a very basic carnal yearning, having taken her by surprise.

There and then she resolved to ensure that nothing further happened and that getting back together with Nigel was the only way forward.

She emerged from her reverie when she realized the air in the room had gone stale and that she hadn't inhaled fresh air for almost two days.

She was overcome with a desire to go for a short, brisk walk to clear the cobwebs in her mind, something she had always done.

She remembered the small park just behind the hotel, pulled a sweater over her head, and walked out toward the park, hopefully without being noticed by anyone. It was a beautiful evening. The air felt fresh on her face and in her lungs. She took deep breaths, exhaling slowly as she quickened her gait. Some children were playing badminton in the park. Couples were strolling, enjoying the breeze, seemingly oblivious to the events unfolding in their country.

She felt a buzz at her belt, and the earpiece in her earring came alive. She saw a picture of an elephant on the screen of her cell phone and knew it was a secure call coming through. Before she could even say hello, a voice started talking to her.

"Dr. Paul, this is Agent John. I work closely with Dave, whom you know. I'm about two hundred feet behind you in a white sweatshirt and black baseball cap. Please, do not make any sudden moves, but turn very slowly to your left and you will see me. Don't make any gestures at me, just keep walking at a normal pace and listen to me very carefully.

"First, you shouldn't have left the hotel—we're a bit disappointed that someone with your experience with us would go out for a walk in these difficult circumstances.

"You may be in danger. Please trust our judgment and do exactly what we tell you or you may not leave this place alive. We've decided to evacuate you and Mr. Surin as soon as possible. If you understand, just turn left and keep walking. Go around the fountain ahead and start back to the hotel. I'll be giving you instructions on what the next steps are."

On approaching the fountain, she glanced casually behind her and saw a dark-haired, moustached, youngish man. She might have seen him several times before in and around the hotel and likely dismissed him as a hotel employee or a taxi driver. She could not see his face clearly.

She continued around the fountain and heard, "That's good. Please go to your room, pack up only the essentials—only what you absolutely have to—and put them in your briefcase. Don't worry about your clothes and personal things. We will arrange to check them and you out of the hotel later and have them delivered to you. We'll be contacting Surin, who will come to your hotel early in the morning. He'll be at the hotel entrance at 4:30 a.m. to drive the two of you in his car to the GA hangar. Enter through the Esso fueling station gate, which will be open. Park the car and walk over to the white-and-green Galaxy twin jet on the ramp.

"Now, I know that you could fly it to a safe destination out of Iran, but under the circumstances, you will not be in the pilot-in-command seat—you can be the co-pilot in the right seat if you like. I've already checked your type-rating on the aircraft, and it's valid. The aircraft computer will be pre-programmed for a direct flight to our destination. The aircraft will depart at 5:30 a.m. sharp, with or without you. I don't need to emphasize this, but absolute secrecy is essential." The phone went dead.

Kevina slowly turned around and saw the same figure in the distance, hurrying toward the park gate.

She needed to get hold of her thoughts. She appreciated that someone was out there watching out for her, but the comfort factor evaporated the moment she remembered his words: "You may be in danger." She felt as if someone had stuck a bull's-eye on her back and was waiting with a sharpshooter's gun, seeking to make his mark. A single shot could easily end it all for her, right then and there. She knew she'd done a silly thing leaving the hotel for a walk, that the situation was serious, and the danger to her real and present, or the JIA wouldn't be wasting time and effort tracking her and making arrangements for her exit.

She thought of Surin and was glad the JIA was going to rescue both of them and take them to safety. The JIA was likely aware of Surin's crucial role in the project. She reminded herself that it was Surin who had really detected the plans of Claude and his cronies. Had he not alerted her to his suspicions, she would quite likely haven't realized in time to be able to do anything about it. She reached the unalterable conclusion that she'd have to ensure his safety because he'd definitely be in danger the moment his role became known to the perpetrators of the coup.

She'd almost reached the hotel gate and noticed there were several taxis waiting. The apparent tranquility was in sharp contrast with the turmoil in her mind. She tried to keep her thinking clear and voice-dialed Surin's number, invoking the secure mode.

"Hi, Kay. In case you're calling for an update, let me tell you there's no problem here. I'm finished preparing our Caviar," Surin said, using their agreed upon codename for the Trojan horse software he'd just successfully implemented in the simulator system. "It's in and looks okay. Only time will tell how good a job we've done. Claude was here and was happy."

"That's great, Surin." She was confident in his ability to ensure his Trojan horse would remain undetected. Should they try to launch their diabolical scheme to infect Iran's air traffic management infrastructure they'd discover their diabolical plan had been thwarted. Undoubtedly, she and Surin would come under suspicion. She didn't want to think any more about the possibilities of events after being caught.

She continued, "But listen: we have to leave for the airport in just a few hours."

"Yes, I was just informed. I have all the details and will be there."

She was happy that JIA was looking after the both of them so well and felt grateful to them for stepping in at the right time to save them.

"Surin, how soon can you be at my hotel? We'll worry about everything else once we reach a safe destination, wherever it is."

Kevina was doing her utmost to convey urgency in her voice. She knew that, like herself, he carried his passport and money in his briefcase—a wise precaution of experienced travellers. He was aware of the definite need to escape from Iran, sooner or later, once their secret mission had been accomplished.

"I need twenty minutes or so before I leave here because I don't want to be seen rushing out in case it arouses suspicion. It's about ten minutes to your hotel from there. I'll be there at the appointed time. Where are going, anyway?"

"I don't know, which is just as well, in case

we're intercepted and don't make it. Remember, in these operations, information is given on a need-to-know basis, because in the end, what you know could come back to haunt you and others.

I'll be waiting downstairs in half an hour, so be careful."

"Okay, see you then." He hung up.

Surin felt his heart pounding in his body. He took the next few minutes to check and process his e-mails. He signed off his account, powered down his tablet, and slowly packed it in its jacket. He removed the passport from his briefcase, stuck it in his other pocket with his wallet, and left the briefcase on the floor next to his desk, visible. He left all his normal office papers where they were. He wanted to convey an I-am-still-around-and-will-be-back look to anyone who might be watching. Now, if only he could slip out and get to his car, unnoticed. He entered the washroom, came out, and went to the cafeteria—there was hardly anyone there—and then to the main entrance. He slowed his pace to a casual gait because he knew the cameras would record his exit as he went through the entrance to the parking lot and approached his car.

He noticed there was another car in the parking lot. At first, he thought someone might be in it, but he paid it no mind, got into his car, and drove off to the hotel to pick up Kevina as casually as possible.

Nigel had just finished the third tennis set of the evening. Since coming to Dubai and while waiting to learn the whereabouts of Kevina, Zoe, and Jim had kept him occupied with tennis and some golf as well. Nigel was grateful for the diversions as they definitely seemed to lower his level of anxiety. That day, however, his mind hadn't been on the game. His first serves had deserted him, as had his backhand. Over the past few years, he'd let his fitness level sink to a new low, and that neglect was manifesting itself in a multitude of aches throughout his body. It seemed all of his muscles had staged a revolt against him in unison. In moments such as these, he'd normally detach himself from the entire world as the ball captivated his being.

Since coming to Dubai, he'd been in a continuous state of quiet desperation. During the day, his ears waited for his phone to ring with a call from Jim with Kevina's whereabouts. At night, he slept badly and had fallen into the trap of clock watching, counting the minutes as they trickled by to bring in a morning that would see definitive information about Kevina. He wondered so many times why it was that human beings had been blessed with an intellect that no other life-form could match when they were also cursed with such a complex mixture of contradictory emotions and inexplicable behavior. Zoe had cautioned him against dwelling on history, suggesting he focus on the present with a definitive and positive plan instead, looking forward to the future with optimism.

He stemmed the thoughts, walked painfully up to his tennis bag, took a towel out, mopped his face, and took a couple of gulps of cold water. He checked his phone and was surprised to note that he'd missed a call from Jim. He used the callback function and was glad to hear Jim's voice.

Jim got to the point. "Nigel, here it is: Kevy is in Tehran. Your hunch was good. She's in a project with the aviation people, so you were right about that, as well."

"Oh, that's a relief."

"But here's the bad news: the entire Iranian airspace is frozen or I would have made arrangements to have you fly in there, ASAP. Anyway, the attempted coup seems to be under control of the government and there's relative calm in the country, generally. So now we believe she's in Tehran, and we know she's safe."

Nigel interrupted, "Any chance of tracking her down and talking to her?"

"My man in Tehran will find out which hotel she's in and see if you can get in touch with her to let her know you're here in Dubai, waiting for her."

"That's good. I'll await your next update. Thanks, Jim. One question, though: should I try to go to Tehran? I'm ready to hop into an aircraft and go there as soon as you tell me."

"No. Definitely no, Nigel. There's no point for you to go on a wild goose chase. The best course of action for you is to stay put here. With the uncertainty there, you likely wouldn't be safe and we'll be going crazy here, worrying over the both of you. Rest assured, we're doing everything to locate her and connect the two of you on the phone. Only then can you plan to go to Tehran. Meanwhile, let the political storm in Iran abate as it seems to be doing. Hopefully, they'll unfreeze the airspace, soon. Continue working on your tennis in the meantime. From what I hear, it needs a lot of work," he said in an attempt to comfort Nigel with humour.

"How soon before you think we'll know her hotel phone number?"

"I think we'll have it tonight or tomorrow,

for sure. Jaff's trying to get it as we speak." Jaff was, in Jim's terminology, his "man in Tehran." Nigel had heard him mention the name often lately.

"Thanks a lot, Jim."

"Okay. I'll see you for dinner in a short while. Remember: we are meeting at the hotel to attend the United States embassy's reception."

Nigel was at the hotel in next to no time at all. He walked through the familiar lobby. The reception was to begin at 7:00 p.m. It was still only 6:00 p.m. As usual, the lobby was very busy—guests checked out, guests checked in, and hotel porters ran to convey baggage to the right rooms. He walked toward the lobby bar and sat behind one of the pillars, shielding himself from the din in front of the lobby. He'd use the hour or so to think of his next moves, now that he could almost feel Kevina's presence next to him.

"Good evening, sir. Can I get you a cocktail?"

He looked up into a friendly, smiling face.

"I'll have a pint of Gulf Dark, please."

He sat at the bar and stared at his watch, watching the minutes tick as he awaited the call from Jim, giving him Kevy's phone number in Tehran. He knew he'd somehow have to communicate to her that he was a different Nigel. He wondered what he would say.

"Kevy, this is a voice you've heard so many times before. Though the voice will sound the same to you, please note that the man uttering these words has finally woken up from a deep and long slumber. Kevy, I've awakened to the full reality of my insensitive ways. I apologize to you for what I haven't done when I should have and could have but simply chose not to. I know why you left me. I've come looking for you and am here to take you back to our home. I cannot go on without you. I simply love you too much to be able to do that. Just say the word, my darling Kevy, and I'll be there immediately."

He rehearsed these lines over and over in his mind. How would she react? He was sure she'd accept his words in a positive light. He wondered if she'd lay down any conditions. It would not matter, even if she did, because no matter what they were, his response would be in the positive.

Nigel remembered the evening almost three decades earlier, when Kevina had walked down the aisle in her stunning, white, wedding dress with her father at the Catholic church. The moment had almost overwhelmed him. They'd been married after a courtship of almost five years. They'd become very serious with each other over the previous twelve months. he had to struggle to keep his composure when he saw her walking toward him. He didn't think anyone had noticed, but tears had welled up in his eyes. She'd noticed his tears the moment she was close to him.

Sipping the ice-cold beer in the bar, he longed to be close to Kevina once more.

# 10

Kevina packed only the bare essentials in her tote bag. She left her clothes hanging in the hotel closet and her suitcase partly closed to leave a lived-in look behind. She put on a full-length coat, wrapped a scarf around her head, and took a last look at herself in the mirror. Yes, she looked somewhat Iranian, she supposed, at least at a casual glance, having been tanned under Tehran's constant sun. She wore her glasses to hide her bluish eyes. She arrived in the deserted lobby. The night-duty receptionist, tired and half-dozing in his seat behind the counter, didn't notice her.

She was about to redial Surin's number when she saw his car pulling up at the lobby entrance. She opened the door and slid into the car with her bag. She looked at Surin and asked, "Is that all you are taking?"

"Well, I could've brought a lot, but they left me no time at all. I don't even have a change of clothes with me. I'm leaving some of my best suits behind for someone else. So, now are you going to tell me exactly what we're up to?"

"Believe me, Surin, you know almost as

much as I do. You agree that after what we've done, we have no choice but to trust Dave, the JIA operative who's awaiting us at the airport? We have to trust the JIA and our governments at this time, as they're trying to help us. So, Surin, I'm putting complete trust in our man, Dave, and suggest you do the same. We really have no other option."

"Is the embassy making the exit arrangements?"

"The embassy's surely involved, but it's the JIA that seems to be managing this affair. I'm sure Dave's made all the arrangements and will look after getting us out, so I have no worries about what they've done. I'm more worried about what might go wrong here, before our takeoff. I'll breathe a sigh of relief when I'm up in the sky," Kevina said.

"There could be other people, as well—what if there isn't enough room for all of us?"

Was Surin jesting to ease the tension, or was that a serious concern? She knew he was a bit of a worrier. Years of managing time-critical developmental projects, especially in designing new, large, software packages, made worriers out of most serious managers. Worry, then, became second nature, and the worrier always looked for things that might go wrong, usually at the worst possible time.

She opted for humor. "That'll be the unluckiest day of your life, won't it?" She patted his hand lightly. "We don't have many options but to hope for the best. Anyway, we'll know within thirty minutes or so."

They sped through the city on the airport expressway. This attempted coup didn't seem to have hit the public as of yet. The population seemed unaware and eerily quiet. The tranquility in the streets was in stark contrast to past upheavals. Widespread demonstrations with considerable, prolonged violence and bloodshed had been common merely a few decades earlier in the country and in the region. It was how opposing factions settled old scores before political settlement could be even contemplated to placate the masses. Perhaps this was just the lull before the storm.

At the airport, the car took a turn toward the Iran Aviation Gas refueling station, pausing at a newly-established checkpoint before the normal GA security checkpoint. It looked as though the new checkpoint had been a reaction to the coup, perhaps in an attempt at some additional security. Kevina noticed it was a manual checkpoint as opposed to the normal, automated checkpoints she'd seen so often.

The security guard, barely visible in the booth, began to bark agitatedly, in Farsi, through the partially open window. Both Kevina and Surin tried hard to catch the gist of his queries but were unsuccessful. They were able to see the refueling station about a hundred yards or so from the checkpoint and the GA office next to it.

They yanked out their passports and placed them on the windowsill in front of the guard. In the light, early morning breeze that caressed the landscape and in the eddies of dust it kicked up, the GA office seemed to recede into the background. Their destination, though physically only a stone's throw away, looked ominously distant and remote. Kevina struggled to remain focused on the present moment and chased the demons of trickery from her tired mind. The security guard switched to English as soon as he saw the Canadian and Indian passports.

"I want you both to sign the visitors' log inside in the security office and walk over to the GA office. No private vehicles are allowed beyond this point. Park over there and then come to the office behind me. Bring all of your bags with you. New procedures have recently been put into place." His English was, thankfully, understandable.

Surin parked the car. Kevina saw rising concern over what awaited them in the security office on his face. He took the bags out, locked the car, and pocketed the electronic key. They grabbed their bags and walked briskly toward security, Kevina leading the way.

She pushed the door of the office open, and a wave of lassitude overcame her. She wished she were somewhere else in that precise moment. For Kevina, this was a rather depressing emotion, and she felt a tightening deep within her stomach. She knew she had to shake the feeling off because escape was near, and she knew she had to be alert, assess the developing situation, and think about solutions to the issues at hand. Hopefully, the JIA was watching her and Surin. She found some comfort in that thought.

Kevina decided she should take the lead. Being a Canadian, she might have more sway with the security people. Surin seemed okay to follow her and let her do all the talking.

Kevina found this security rigmarole a bit annoying, but given the developing situation in the country, it wasn't totally unwarranted. She tried to rationalize it in her mind. After all, there had been a coup attempt, and as a result, the normally tight security had to be beefed up even more.

They'd both already been biometrically scanned and everything about them would be displayed on the screen behind the scanners. They placed their palmtops in the tray before entering the magnetic and x-ray scanners, proceeded through them, and awaited the return of their equipment.

Kevina was surprised to hear a familiar voice.

"Well, well, well. Fancy finding you both here. So, where are you folks off to? Could it be that you're leaving us unannounced? No, that's just impossible. I mean, there's so much work still to do, and I know how conscientious the two of you are."

Kevina instantly recognized Claude's distinct voice and the laughter that followed, which cut through the still air and went straight to her heart.

Kevina spun around, and she saw Surin do the same. The sun's rays streamed through a small window in the wall, illuminating dust particles suspended in the still air in the dark, little cubicle. She looked up to face Claude. Her eyes locked on his prominent Adam's apple and the sneer above it. Behind him were two armed, heavyset, stony guardsmen.

"Oh, hi, Claude. Might I ask what you're doing here?" Surin asked, faking a smile, obviously trying his best to sound as casual as possible. Surin's interjection gave Kevina some time to think.

She took the cue and said, "We came here hoping to rent an aircraft to do some local flying. You know both of us have to keep flying or our validities lapse. We'll do a couple of hours this evening." She was sure she sounded unconvincing, but it was the best she could come up with.

"I have bad news for the two of you lovebirds: the airspace is frozen under current national circumstances. Only specially authorized military aircraft can fly. Why am I telling you all this? Surely, you know. Surely you're aware there's been a disruption in the government here," he said in a voice deep in sarcasm.

"Pleasure GA flying? Come on. You must be kidding. There's just no way. I can assure you will not get approval to do any flying at all."

Claude continued in his slow, deliberately exaggerated, polite manner. "But guess what? I have a small request for the two of you: I respectfully request you to come to the centre for a short while to clear up something which has cropped up that confounds us. We need to consult with you for a short time."

"I'm sure we can be at the centre tomorrow morning with the full team to analyze and resolve whatever issue's come up," Kevina said. "I know, for sure, there's nothing urgent outstanding."

Betraying a hint of annoyance, Claude turned to look directly at Kevina. "Yes, but there's an even more important task that I have, and that's to ensure your safety in these troubled times. I've been asked specifically by our senior VP to ensure you two are safe during the current upheaval. That's the main reason you should be with me. And as long as we're together, we might as well do some work, given the critical stage we're at in the development of the project.

"Cheer up, Dr. Paul. Don't look so disappointed. An hour or so max with us and I'll personally make sure I get you back to safety. Meanwhile, I'll see how I can assist you in getting the clearance to fly so you can have your picnic in the air. I'm confident I'll be able to arrange it for you while you're with me. Think of this as just a short a delay before your aerial jolly. Please follow these two gentlemen who'll provide us all with an armed escort. I'll be right with you in the van."

Claude laughed, picked up their palmtops, and placed them in his bag. "You won't be needing these toys for a short time. I assure you they're safe with me. You'll get them back very shortly."

Kevina found her voice and said, "Claude, I'd like to talk to the VP. Can I do that now, please? You know I'm directly responsible to him, per my contract."

"Dr. Paul, right now I have a higher calling, and that's getting you two to safety. Once that's done, you can talk to whomever you want. Right now, we need to get going without delay. Please follow us."

The two armed men positioned themselves behind Kevina and Surin, leaving little doubt as to who was the focus of their attention. Kevina and Surin exchanged glances, communicating the hopelessness of the situation and the need to obey Claude and his gang of goons; there was no other way.

The short walk to the waiting van seemed long. Kevina's mind worked feverishly to find a way out. She also hoped Surin would maintain his cool. They got into the middle seat. Claude sat next to the driver, with his armed cronies in the seat behind Surin and Kevina. Kevina recognized the harsh reality upon them. They were effectively Claude's prisoners—there was no other way to describe their current situation. How dramatically events had changed in the last few moments. Kevina sighed deeply. She knew Dave would become aware of their situation in due course, but how long would it take? Without her palmtop, she was cut off from communicating their predicament to him. She felt as though one of her arms had gone missing. She tried to remember but could not recall when she was last without her palmtop and totally incommunicado from the world.

The van sped along the airport expressway toward the city. Claude busied himself on the phone in a long, drawn-out, and often agitated conversation with someone in Farsi. Finally, Claude stopped talking on the phone and barked instructions at the driver.

"Where are we are going?" Surin asked with concern.

"Where else, my friend, but to the centre?"

Kevina looked outside and tried to focus on where they were headed. The en route traffic appeared normal. Obviously, the coup seemed confined, and there was relief in that, though there appeared to be more of a police presence on the roads than normal—or was that simply her imagination? Her train of thought was interrupted when she sighted the centre, and the van pulled up to the main entrance.

From the back of the van, Claude's bodyguards—or more appropriately, his goons—jumped out, opened the doors, and gestured for her and Surin to follow Claude. Before Claude was able to touch the doorknob for bio-recognition and for the entrance to open, Kevina heard a noise. She turned to see the two bodyguards behind her slumping forward and collapsing on the pavement. She saw three heavily armed, uniformed, Iranian army soldiers with Tasers in their hands, shouting at Claude in Farsi.

On seeing his goons collapse, Claude put his arms up in the air, palms open, looking at Kevina with pleading eyes. Two soldiers dragged the two stunned bodyguards away to a waiting van, while a third one took custody of Claude, handcuffed him, and gently nudged him toward a military car. Claude looked devastated, seeming to age in those moments, his posture drooping, his gait wobbly. In front of them, the centre door opened from inside, and a man stepped out and approached them with his hand pointing to another car in the parking lot. Kevy felt this had to be Dave Summers.

"Hi, folks. Sorry for that Taser display—quite terrible, actually, but unfortunately, purely business. Let me assure you, this is not my favorite part of my job. I actually hate fisticuffs. Please turn around, and let's walk over to that car immediately. Don't worry about your companions. The army folks will have a friendly chat with them when they wake up. They'll recover from their headaches in a half hour or so. Thanks to modern technology, they'll all be fine, I'm sure. As far as your pal's concerned, he's going to realize soon that we're all fully aware he was up to no good, and he'll have some explaining to do."

Kevy and Surin exchanged glances as they hurried toward the car. Dave quickly ran around them, reached the car, and held the door open for them to get in. He sat in the front next to the driver, and the car rolled out of the parking lot.

The entire exchange had taken less than a couple of minutes from the time they'd hopped out of Claude's car. Kevina felt a sense of relief. The transition from being in Claude's care to Dave's care was sudden, and of course, quite welcome. She put her hand on Surin's and gave it a comforting squeeze. She looked at Dave and said, "Thanks, Dave. Just in time. I had no idea what was going to happen to us."

From the time they'd arrived at the newly set-up security gate to the appearance of Dave with the soldiers had been less than five minutes.

Dave simply waved his hand. "Well, it's difficult to say what he had in store for you, but I feel you'd have been a bit uncomfortable. Thank your lucky stars that you guys have been in my care so far. I will be free of that worry and move on to my next project, pretty soon. It's all a game for me, you see. The risks we take in my business for our protégés sometimes amaze me. The good thing is that people like me will always have jobs because the demand is so great and growing each month." He laughed.

"Anyway, now we're indeed going to the airport, and I'm going to make sure nothing goes wrong. Here are your palmtops, by the way." Dave gave both of the palmtops to Kevina who kept her own and passed the second one to Surin. She saw that Dave was already busy with his own palmtop, tapping away.

Kevy knew he was likely making a quick report, planning his next move. His demeanor was such that it discouraged any further questions or conversation. It was another five minutes before they arrived at the airport and went through the automatic security gate.

Dave said, "Dr. Paul and Mr. Surin, please continue walking directly to the Super Galaxy. The door's open. Leave your bags under the wing and I'll take care of them. Mr. Surin, please get in first, in the backseat. Dr. Paul, climb in the right front seat, buckle in, relax, and I'll come around."

Kevina walked to the aircraft, her trained eyes noting the unusual configuration of the special-purpose aircraft. While not quite a military aircraft, it was equipped with pods that carried surveillance, jamming, and defensive capabilities. She knew the various high-technology sensing systems would keep an automatic lookout for dangers the Galaxy might encounter when in the air. Below the wings, she noticed the weaponry, able to deploy either automatically or manually by the pilot. There was only one word to describe the defense and assault capabilities of this ultramodern aircraft: awesome.

The jamming systems would detect any enemy airborne or ground radar trying to track or follow the Galaxy. The system would jam the radar to avoid detection by making the aircraft invisible to enemy radar systems, disabling their ability to track its flight path. The aircraft could then continue its journey in stealth mode. The onboard radar and laser surveillance systems kept electronic vigil in the airspace around the aircraft to ensure that no suspicious airborne vehicle would approach the Galaxy without first alerting the pilot. Inside the cockpit, the threat assessment computer would display a picture of the airspace around it for the pilot, identifying friendly and enemy aircraft in proximity, and proposing strategies to thwart any menacing actions. The intelligence encoded in the software also guarded against erroneous discharge of weapons, including missiles and laser weapons. Meanwhile, the system kept continuous contact with the JIA control centre, providing regular updates on the progress of the aircraft once it was airborne.

The Galaxy aircraft engines roared into life and settled down to a metallic whine. The aircraft rolled ahead toward the button of the takeoff runway. The scopes and displays in the cockpit came alive. Kevina glanced at the navigation display and noted the aircraft's initial flight path was projected in a southerly direction. Critical information was displayed on a heads-up display on the Galaxy's windscreen. A few minutes later, the Galaxy accelerated, leaped off the runway into the air, and settled in its pre-programmed track to the destination, known only to the pilot, Dave Summers.

When Kevina could no longer contain her anxiety, she said, "All right, Dave. Where are we headed? Do you intend to blindfold us?" She tried to laugh to lighten the tension.

"No, that won't be necessary, at least, not at this time. My mission is to take you and your pal to Dubai. Arrangements are being made as we speak to ensure you get processed through immigration without any problem. Assuming that all goes off as planned and you're not charged with illegal entry and get marched off to the local prison, you're to walk straight outside, where a black limo will be waiting. Walk to it slowly, wait for the uniformed chauffeur to greet you both by name, and then and only then, get into the limo. You'll receive more instructions from then on.

"I know do one thing: they don't want either of you to go back to Canada or the United States—too many people know you there, and HQ thinks you and your loved ones, assuming you have some, will be in mortal danger. So, with these caveats in mind, you'll have to figure out where you should go from Dubai. If I were you, I'd look at South Asia or East Asia, not that it concerns me."

Sarcasm was second nature to Dave. It seemed that was how people like him dealt with situations involving life and death—by trivializing them and enveloping them in humor. Perhaps, in his business, detaching oneself from the situation was the only way to survive.

Kevina knew Dave had to go through some very rigorous training, observing situations unfolding before him, looking for clues, and piecing it all into comprehensible stories. Dave looked like a seasoned operative, used to working in solitude, even though electronically, he was closely connected to his office advisors and analysts of all descriptions.

People like Dave handled a lot of information about a lot of people—good and bad. During their training, they were coached on how to guard information, use it, and give it out only to those who were cleared, and even then on a need-to-know basis. This is how they protected themselves, others, and the entire system. They seldom doled out advice, did what needed to be done, and informed those involved only when absolutely necessary—and even then, only minimally. Dave's all-knowing but inaccessible attitude wrapped in sarcasm discouraged further queries.

Kevina looked at Surin who stared back with a stoic expression. He posed no questions, and neither did she. It appeared there was no point in asking any questions. It would be futile to try to penetrate the fortress of information in Dave's skull.

Kevina determined there was really no option but to live in the moment, trust Dave and his organization, and handle events as they unfolded. She looked out into the blue sky. The tension inside her started to dissipate when she turned to introspection as she normally did whenever she felt worn out. After all, where would she and Surin be without their intervention? She glanced back. Surin had his eyes closed, indicating a quiet acceptance of the situation they were in—maybe it was just as well.

She knew she'd have to look into the future and determine her actions, and the first question was in front of her. Where would she go now that she wasn't able to return home? Back to Nigel?

Nigel's one-line note appeared and lingered in her mind. When she'd left him earlier, she had no earlier doubt she was doing the right thing, but now, going back to him was clearly a good option, and she really wanted to.

"One more thing for you guys. Please listen carefully." Dave's monotone voice broke the silence in the aircraft cockpit. "You've likely figured this out, if not, then in time I'm sure you'll realize you've played a significant role in foiling what might have been a major, regional, cyber-terrorism plot. The implications may be far reaching, possibly global, but we may not know the full extent for some time. Unfortunately, effective immediately, you won't be able to brag about this to your friends, or even mention it to anyone. The entire operation has been accorded the highest security designation for the next thirty years—it's classified at a JIA ultra-secret level, which makes it a crime to even think about it." He let out another guffaw.

His sarcasm continued, "Rest assured, this story will never make it to CNN. All reference to the event and this trip will be removed from all JIA records. What you've done and what you've been through will remain buried in the unwritten record, never to be revealed. This kills any plans you may have to write a book and make millions on it for at least thirty years, and likely, not even then. Am I making this clear?"

Both Kevina and Surin said, "Yes, understood."

"Unfortunately, this is the fate of most good stories and the good work people like you and I do. No one will ever write or even talk about what we achieve. We do our stuff, and you have no idea what planning and effort have gone into our mission to save the two of you. If we succeed, our deeds simply get buried in the junk of history, but our failures—and we do have a few—gain publicity and get written indelibly into public history, only to make us look like incompetent, bumbling idiots with evil schemes to victimize faraway lands and innocent people. The media feeds on our failures and ignores our successes. I'm not sure whether history will do anything different." His bitterness broke through the exterior facade of a cool, disconnected professional.

Kevina felt that in Dave—if that was his real name—deep down, there likely was some humanity concealed behind his outward toughness.

Don't we all crave for recognition from our fellow beings? Yes, Dave was right in his observation of the stories behind his activities, though she hadn't had occasion to think about it until then. She'd have a great story to tell that would interest many people, and she'd have liked to at least have the choice. In the long run, someday she'd have even liked to have written about her adventure in Iran. She thought about Surin and felt a warmth coming over her, but she knew that she had to filter the episode with him out of her life. It was just happenstance, and that was it, nothing more. She felt she had to eradicate most events of the last day or so from her memory.

She looked out the window and admired the scenery unfolding below them. As the sun dipped over the western skies, she saw all of southern Iran, the Persian Gulf, and the southern part of Afghanistan through a blanket of bluish-gray haze. The greenish-brown mountains below merged into the bluish-green waters of the Persian Gulf. It was beautiful and tranquil, masking the upheaval that was occurring down below in many people's lives. A coup in a country like Iran—even an attempted coup—would have unpleasant, life-altering impact on a lot of people. Would the moderate president survive? Would the people they knew and left behind survive? She saw some optimism in that the army seemed to be loyal to the current president. After all, it was the army that had rescued them from the clutches of Claude and his goons. Also, it appeared as though Dave was working with the current president. Did he enjoy the full support of the Iranian army or just a faction? It was so difficult to gauge the present and forecast the future in a country like Iran.

# 11

Surin thought of Kevy. It was difficult for him to shake off what had happened the previous night. He could still feel her arms around him. Now, in the cockpit, he wondered if he should reach over and touch her shoulder. He wanted to say so much to her, but he knew he had to overcome the desire. He'd have to choose a more appropriate moment, hopefully one in the near future.

His forced his mind to drift away onto another track, thinking about his home in Bengaluru. He missed home, but he was too busy trying to make sense of what Dave was saying, what had happened, and Kevy. He knew he'd have to map out his future path carefully. If they couldn't go back to Canada or the United States, then the only possibility was to go back to Bengaluru. Would Kevina go with him? The thought warmed him all over. He would, of course, try his best to convince her, and he hoped it would be easy to do so.

"Tell me, Dave: how were Claude's sabotage scheme and the coup related? Of course, the coincidence is something that makes you wonder, but I can't figure out how the two could be linked," Surin heard Kevina saying.

"What I'm able to tell you is that we've been tracking Claude and his gang for some time now. They're members of a sleeper cell of one of the extremist groups in the region. The cell's a part of a group that's been financing terrorist activities in the region. I can't tell you more, mostly because we're not sure ourselves, but we know this particular group's specialty is cyber-terrorism. We're really concerned this cell's recruited a few very-well-qualified and experienced but ill-intentioned cyber-security specialists who are using their skills to illegally hack into business, personal, and government sites."

Surin knew about cyber- and high-tech terrorists. Their specialty had been to disrupt international power grids and to penetrate data networks and the like. These people had also tried to disrupt several refineries. Any modern, processor-controlled factory, refinery, or power plant would be vulnerable to external interference from distant locations. While it was not easy to hack into these establishments, it was possible in the hands of a skilled hacker. With the availability of unlimited time and computing power combined with an expertise to develop special hacking software, a hacker could, with a bit of luck, find a way to penetrate defenses and create havoc. Over time, some of their evil forays had even been notably successful.

Dave continued, "We didn't have anything concrete on them, so when you began unearthing their plans to disrupt the ATC system, it all fit right in, and the overall picture became clearer to us. HQ normally doesn't get too excited over people calling us from all corners of the world claiming to have uncovered nefarious schemes of imagined terrorists, as a vast majority of them are without foundation. It takes mere minutes to dismiss them. Interestingly, your story took mere minutes to corroborate with what we already knew of your friend. And, of course, the coup complicated everything.

"Then the mission of saving you was assigned and became my most important challenge. Thanks to our sophisticated, highly accurate, and very quiet Tasers, we were able to Tase the characters from quite a distance, quickly rendering them immobile. My number-one concern was that if they had even a few seconds' warning of our presence, they'd surely have killed you. They'd have considered it a success for them, even if they had to die for it."

The landing at Dubai was routine. They were whisked through customs and immigration formalities and taken to Dubai Metro Hotel in a special car. There, they went to their assigned rooms and simply crashed, tired from lack of sleep and the tension of the past thirty-odd hours.

The next morning, Surin was already in the coffee shop waiting for Kevina. He knew Dave would come around, as well. Before long he saw Kevina emerge from the elevator and head straight for his table.

She looked relaxed. The expression of worry she'd worn for the past few days was gone, and she looked younger than she had in days. He watched as she approached his table, seeming to glide across the fairly large restaurant in easy and graceful strides; her gait confident and elegant. Her hair bouncing, caressing her cheeks, the whisper of a smile on her lips, her body erect, her head held high on her slender neck. She was dressed in a pair of light-blue slacks reaching just below her knees and a pink shirt fitting snugly on her upper body, doing full justice to her fine physique. She looked stunning.

She looked straight at Surin, and he wondered if she was able to read his thoughts. As she approached his table, he rose. She kissed him lightly on his cheek and sat in the chair next to him. "I haven't slept like that for a long time. You look refreshed. I hope you slept as well as I did," she said.

Was she a bit distant? Surin wasn't sure, but he nodded in agreement and said, "Look, Kevy, after you retired last night, I spent a few minutes with Dave Summers, who should be down in about a half hour or so. Dave assured me that we're both safe here and free to go almost anywhere except North America, at least for the time being. So I spent few minutes on my laptop, and here's what I have done."

With that, he opened his briefcase took out two airline e-tickets. "Kevy, we're going this evening to Bengaluru. I've already taken the liberty of booking a passage for you, as well. You heard what that guy told us: both of us have to go to a place where we'll be safer. You certainly won't be able to go back home for at least the next few weeks. You just can't afford to take the risk of going to North America and exposing yourself to personal danger. Dubai's safe for us, Dave confirmed it. Let's face it: its proximity to Iran should be a concern, despite all the assurances."

Surin remembered she'd told him that her grandfather's father was Indian, but she didn't have any details. She'd said she knew nothing about her great-grandfather, and that she hadn't seriously looked into this element of her genealogy to it. Surin hoped he was making sense to her and that she'd at least consider what he was saying.

He continued, "So I have the perfect plan for you: come with me to India, only for a while, till the dust settles. You'll be safe in my world and then go back to yours. A long time ago, you told me you had some Indian blood in you. You also mentioned you'd one day like to know more about that side of you. Kevina, here's a unique and highly opportune moment to experience a whole new, different world. Come experience our hospitality."

"My, that is quite compelling, Surin. You should be in tourism promotion for India. But right now, I'm starving and need some food. Only then will I be able to think more about my safety and immediate plan."

"Okay. This is a buffet breakfast, so why don't we pick up what we want and get back here?"

Surin saw her pick up a bowl, fill it with assorted cereals, top it with honey and crushed flaxseeds, pour herself an herbal tea, and return to her chair. Surin was a bit slower.

Had he tried to sell the idea of going to India too aggressively? Was he pushing it throwing the tickets in her face? Women like Kevina didn't get pushed around too easily. Maybe he should tell her he went a bit overboard there. "You're a smart woman," he should say. "You know the issues. Figure out your next set of actions and I'll be on my way. Let me know if you want to come with me."

He grabbed a bagel and egg sandwich and a

cup of coffee and hurried back to his table.

He started, "Look, Kevy—"

He couldn't finish because he heard her say, "I've done some thinking, as well, and I'm inclined to agree with you. I have no other ready options. I've always wanted to go to India, and maybe this is my chance. We'll depart this evening, as you say, but with one very important requirement: I'd like to stay in a hotel, hopefully not too far from your residence. I may also do some touring and shopping on my own."

Surin was silent for a few minutes as he contemplated what Kevy had said. He knew he didn't have a choice, but hiding his disappointment as best as he could, he said, "Sure, Kevy. Whatever's comfortable for you is fine with me. I am, of course, delighted you've agreed to spend some time in Bengaluru. You have your e-ticket—I can easily confirm the hotel reservation for you in the next couple of hours.

"Go and see the touristy spots, but as a part of a group organized and managed by the hotel. Please don't venture out alone at night except on conducted tours. As far as shopping's concerned, I'm sure the hotel's reception desk will guide you and may even recommend a taxi to take you around safely. Bengaluru is generally a safe place, and the people tend to be quite nice, but bad things have happened and do still happen. Keeping in mind all that's happened here, we both have to be very cautious. I'm sure you know that, but enjoy yourself."

Kevy assured him she'd pay heed to his counsel. She told him that as a worldwide traveller, she'd always been careful and that she wouldn't throw caution to the wind.

They continued working through breakfast at a leisurely pace. Surin wanted to tell her the previous night definitely had not been a one-night affair for him, and that, in fact, he wasn't that type. He wondered if he should tell her the significance the other night had for him, going forward. He'd be straightforward and tell her he'd be delighted if she were to consider him an option, moving forward in her life. He'd become aware there had been a recent fracture in her relationship with her husband.

He really wanted to tell her, "Look, just enjoy Bengaluru and its environs, and while I am available, if you want to go anywhere you're under no obligation of any kind to include me in any of your activities while in India or beyond. But for the long term, I'd be delighted to be a part of your life once you've sorted out your situation in Canada." He thought, and prudently so, that he should wait for the right signal from her before he expressed his thoughts.

While he'd continue to wait for a signal from her, he couldn't help but wonder if she, too, were waiting for a sign from him. A pregnant silence hung between them, punctuated by sounds of munching. Surin stood up to go to the beverage bar to get another coffee. Kevy continued eating her cereal and sipped her tea. He glanced toward Kevina from the beverage bar, to see she was tapping a message on her palmtop.

Kevina thought it the right time to let Nigel know of her plans, and she tapped out a short message to Nigel on her palmtop:

*Nigel,*

*I'm safe and will be so in Bengaluru. After tomorrow, please come immediately to the Maharaja Hotel in Bengaluru. First, get a tourist visa for India and book your flight. Please send me your flight details, ASAP.*

*Look forward to seeing you in Bengaluru.*

*Kevy*

Surin came back with a full plate and a mug of coffee. He looked at Kevy and said, "I just got a message from my company, which is now aware of what's happened. People there want me to stop over in Delhi for one night and then go to Bengaluru. I just consulted with Dave—why don't you come with me to Delhi? You could do a tour of the city, and we could continue to Bengaluru the next day, as planned. I'll take another direct flight to Delhi and see you at the hotel a day later. We can easily change your reservations right at the airport."

"Surin, I understand the situation fully. Who knows? While in Delhi, your office may want to extend your stay to brief the appropriate Indian government offices, as well. So, please, go ahead, and I will, as currently planned, go to Bengaluru.

"Also, Surin, there's something I must discuss with you, about what happened last night between you and I. We both must put it behind us and consider it happenstance, and while I won't forget those moments with you, we must both consider it a dead end that won't go anywhere. Indeed, there's no future in it, whatsoever. You're a wonderful young man, but your future's not with me, please recognize that. You know I'm married. My husband will be joining me very soon, most likely in Bengaluru."

Surin put his fork down and looked out the window, a bit shocked.

She continued, "Surin, you remember meeting Nigel a few years back at our company Christmas? I think you both seemed to get along well. This will be a good chance to renew that link."

"Okay, Kevy, whatever you say. I fully respect your wishes. Rest assured that while I'll cherish that brief time with you, I won't mention it ever again, to you or to anyone else. I do hope, though, that this doesn't mean that we won't ever meet again."

"Not at all. I'll definitely await your arrival in a day or two in Bengaluru and meet with you as friends. In any event, while I await Nigel's arrival, I'll likely spend the first couple of days relaxing, taking stock of the situation, finding out all I can about those conducted tours you mentioned, working out, and so on."

She saw Dave approach their table.

Dave said, "Good morning. Hope you had a restful night."

Kevy thought his arrival was great timing for her. She'd wanted to end the dialogue with Surin in a nice manner. She motioned for Dave to sit down and said, "Yes. Thank you, again. We'll never forget what you've done for us, Dave. How about you? Did you have a restful night?" "Oh, I hardly slept. Today, my plan is to stay in my room, catch up on my sleep, and await instructions for my next project."

"Were you busy making your reports to

HQ?"

"Yes, and also making sure you're safe while here and that someone will tell us when to move from here, unless you want to extend your stay."

"I believe Surin has spoken to you about going to Bengaluru for a few days. I believe you're okay with that? My husband will most likely join me there in the next couple of days. Then, yes, I'll want to get back home to Toronto."

"That's fine."

Dave looked at Surin and said, "For you, it'll be a homecoming, so you must be happy. I'm starved right now. Let me get some breakfast. Can I get anything for either of you?" Both of them shook their heads, and Dave made his way to the buffet.

Surin checked on his palmtop and got a direct Dubai to Delhi flight. When Dave came back with a full plate, Surin stood up.

"I'd better go, get ready, and proceed to the airport. Not that I have much to take since I arrived with only a small shoulder bag. So this is it, folks. Goodbye, for the time being. I'll see you both in Bengaluru in a day or so. Dave, once again, thanks for all you've done to save our lives. I'll never forget it. I'll keep you both informed." He turned to Kevina and said, "Dr. Paul, I hope I'll see you in Bengaluru at the Maharaja Hotel with your husband, and maybe we can go out for a couple of dinners?"

"Absolutely, Surin. I'll call you for sure, and we'll look forward to spending several evenings with you. I know Nigel will be pleased to meet you again."

Surin offered his hand to Kevina, shook it, and then shook Dave's hand. He turned around and walked to the elevator, likely to go to his room, pick up his bag, and rush off to the airport.

Shortly thereafter, Kevina saw Surin leaving the hotel from her seat in the restaurant. She felt this change in Surin's itinerary was indeed convenient for her and was just as well. She felt happy at how she'd handled their parting as well. She felt she'd been clear in terms of putting the recent past in the right context as well as their future relationship with Nigel around. She was also pleased with the manner in which he'd responded. She was impressed with Surin's professional and mature understanding of the situation.

She turned to Dave and asked, "Dave, what are your plans while in Bengaluru...or are you not allowed to discuss that with me?" She laughed.

"Well, I'll have a lot to catch up with a few of our people there, but I'll try to hook up with you and your hubby and Surin for a meal or two. Don't worry about me. When I'm free, I'll call you to see if we can set something up. You know, I've been to Bengaluru many times, but I've never once gone sightseeing or even shopping, so who knows? I may do that with both of you."

They finished their breakfasts in silence, skimming through the newspapers left on the table, noting they were full of news of the coup attempt in Iran, but with little new information. She checked to see if there was any mention of aviation systems. The paper did state that Iranian airspace had been frozen and only a few flights with prior, military approval were being permitted to operate in and out of Tehran, but there was nothing other than that, which was just as well with Kevina and Dave.

After breakfast and a quick goodbye, she walked over to the hotel gym in the basement, pleased to see it was well equipped.

A half hour later, she was in the gym. She jogged on the treadmill, pumped some iron, stretched, and took a shower. She felt energized and ready for her flight to Bengaluru. She checked her watch to find she had plenty of time to check out, head to the airport, and maybe browse around the Dubai airport, which was famous for its world-class shopping facilities.

# 12

Nigel tried making idle chit-chat with some of the faces he recognized at the embassy reception that evening. There was a lot of buzz about the coup in Tehran. Though it clearly hadn't been successful, the government was not in full control and there was a lot of chaos in the country. The airport in Tehran was still with the rebel group, which, it was being said, was affiliated with ultra-right-wing fanatics who wanted to overturn the progress Iran had made over the past decade. Nigel absorbed as much information as he could while his eyes searched for Jim. At last, he saw him in the entrance. He waved at Jim who met Nigel at the bar. He ordered a glass of red wine and threw Jim a questioning look.

"Just talked to Jaff, and he's located Kevy in Tehran at the Hotel Intercontinental. Jaff says she's not in her room, and he'd already gone to the hotel to find her. He's going to stay there till he finds her. Here, Nigel, are Kevy's hotel phone and room numbers. You can call her right now if you like. She is not there, but you could leave her a message. Alternatively, you could wait till Jaff locates her and proceed from there. He should be—"

Nigel was already dialing the number. "Kevy, darling, it's me, Nigel," he said into the phone. "I want you to know I love you, and please call me immediately. I'm in Dubai." He left his phone number and signed off from the voicemail.

"Jim, what's our embassy's position on the whole Iran affair?" he asked.

"What I just told you is mostly from the embassy. They told me one more thing: they're tracking her because she's been keeping them informed of her activities."

"What activities? What are they talking about?"

"I couldn't get any more out of my contact. Obviously, she's involved in some project that holds the embassy's interest. Her project seems to be shrouded in secrecy, but the good thing is they're keeping an eye on her and her safety."

Nigel was aware Kevina had been involved in mission-critical secret projects several times in the past. Now he wondered what kind of secret activity in Iran could possibly be of interest to the Canadian embassy. Was her activity in any way involved with the coup? Was her presence in the country associated with a secret project linked to the national coup, or were those mere coincidences?

"Will the embassy fly her out of Iran, do you think?" Nigel asked, knowing it to be a redundant question.

"I don't know that right now, but I'm sure they'll do all they can. My contact knows I'm concerned about her and will keep me advised to the extent he can." At least, that's what Jim had hoped.

"Anyway, I've got to run. Nigel, have no doubt that I'm on top of this situation. I'll call you the second I know something." He left quickly with a business associate—likely for a quiet dinner, or that's what Nigel guessed.

Nigel hung around, snacking on hors d'oeuvres. He felt alone, though he was surrounded by quite a few people. He wished Kevy were there with him. He heard his palmtop buzzing and flipped it open to see a message:

*Nigel,*

*I'm safe and will be so in Bengaluru. After tomorrow, please come immediately to the Maharaja Hotel in Bengaluru. First, get a tourist visa for India and book your flight. Please send me your flight details ASAP.*

*Looking forward to seeing you in Bengaluru.*

*Kevy*

His heartbeat increased. He called Zoe to tell her about the e-mail.

"I'm so glad she's safe. Bengaluru, you say? That might be fun. I wonder why not Toronto...Anyway, Nigel, I can help you with the Indian visa and booking the flight out. I'm sure you could be on your way to her tomorrow. Jim's already on his way here. We can talk over dinner. Did you tell her where you are? If not, do so immediately, so she knows you've been trying to follow her, that's very important, Nigel."

"Yes, of course. And Zoe: I'll take a cab and come to your house right away and start packing for tomorrow."

He walked out of the embassy party, which appeared to be in full swing. After a couple of thank-yous to the hosts, he hopped into a waiting cab, and a half hour later, he was at their house and being greeted by Zoe.

He was excited, quite excited, indeed—he was going to meet Kevy in India. Who would have thought that one day after their estrangement they'd meet in Bengaluru to make up and press their relationship's reset button? What an incredible turn of events!

He sent her an e-mail:

*Kevy,*

*I'm actually already in Dubai with Zoe and Jim. I should be able to get the flight to Bengaluru, most likely tomorrow, direct from Dubai. I'm on to the visa process and airline reservations and will let you know, ASAP.*

*Really looking forward to seeing you.*

*Love,*

*Nigel*

He wanted to say a lot more, but he decided to save his outpouring of love and affection for a tête-à-tête with her. Kevy seemed to have clearly left the door ajar and now it was up to him. He felt encouraged by her invitation. He didn't care where he'd have to go to see her. This was the time to show her how he felt about her, and he was determined to show her he realized the error of his ways and had completely changed.

Nigel went to his room and started packing for his journey to India—his first ever. By dinnertime, the ever-efficient Zoe had worked out all of the steps for his departure to Bengaluru.

Later, he went to the dining room, where Zoe was waiting for him. "Tomorrow, you and I will go to the Indian embassy," she said. "I know the trade attaché quite well, thanks to Jim, and have already talked to him. He expects us with your passport at 9:30 a.m. He's promised he'll have the tourist visa for you without any trouble."

"Thanks so much, Zoe."

"I'm afraid you'll have to spend one more night with us and take the early morning flight the day after tomorrow, direct to Bengaluru. It shouldn't take more than two hours or so from here. Jim and I know the Maharaja Hotel—it's truly great. I've arranged for the hotel limo to pick you up at the airport and take you to the Maharaja. I think this is the best for you. Both of you will be fresh, and you can spend the whole day talking. Though, I do hope you'll be doing most of the talking to bring your relationship back on the rails."

Nigel found little to disagree with her.

Over dinner, Jim and Zoe talked a lot about their visit to Bengaluru. Jim had been there on business several times but had seen very little of the countryside, as he had to shuttle between the hotel room and boardrooms. A year or so earlier, he and Zoe had a short vacation there and had really enjoyed themselves. One of the highlights of their trip was a visit to the Ajanta Caves. To do that, they had to fly north to Aurangabad to catch their limo tour of the Ajanta Caves.

"If you have the time, maybe you and Kevy could spend at least a full day there. Take a conducted tour and walk around and see the beauty of the paintings, sculptures, and art from the ancient Buddhist culture. If I remember correctly, the paintings are some twenty-three hundred years old."

"Well, we might have a few days. I'll definitely mention this to Kevy."

Jim continued, "The caves were kind of lost for over fifteen hundred years till a Brit army guy, John Smith, discovered them in the early nineteenth century, had them excavated, and revealed them to the world. The construction of the caves is a bit of an engineering puzzle. You will find it very interesting.

"Some thirty caves were excavated to store the first Buddhist monuments from the second century BCE. For the next five or six centuries, Hindu kings added many statues and paintings, all of which gives us some understanding of their life—at least from the Buddhist point of view—and more importantly, before the Islamic period in India. I do think Kevy will find the caves and the sculptures and paintings quite interesting. I understand she has some Indian blood in her. Was her grandmother partly Indian?"

"Actually, it was her great-grandfather who was Indian and who immigrated to Canada from Africa. I'll surely mention your recommendation to Kevy and make it a point to see them."

Zoe jumped into the discussion. "That's all very interesting, but don't forget what your priority ought to be in Bengaluru when you see Kevy. There'll be plenty of time for all of this touristy stuff and more."

As soon as the flight had been booked, Nigel sent Kevy an e-mail.

*Kevy,*

*Am hoping to get my visa tomorrow in the morning, but my flight to Bengaluru is booked for the day after tomorrow: ETA Bengaluru 0900 Flight JJ230.*

*See you at your hotel at about 10:00, the day after tomorrow.*

*Nigel*

The next morning, Zoe maneuvered Nigel through the Indian embassy's visa office deftly and expertly. Within an hour or so at the embassy, she had a six-month tourist visa stamped on Nigel's Canadian passport. Nigel quickly realized the great relationship Jim and Zoe enjoyed with the embassy staff.

In the car on the way home from the embassy, Nigel looked at Zoe and said, "I know I'll need to make a real and lasting first impression on Kevy when we meet. I want to make it memorable, something that will please her besides my words, something that she can always look at and say to herself was the tipping point in the new beginning in our relationship. I know she won't be impressed with some expensive gift, but she'd appreciate a symbolic gesture. Right now I'm thinking about what that might be."

"If I could make a suggestion, it would be to buy her a wedding ring and present it as the symbolic gesture you're looking for. But as I've said before, your opening words to her are the most important, and then, of course, the actions. The attitude and long-term behaviour will back the words up."

That was it. He knew which ring he'd get her. It couldn't be anything ostentatious—that definitely wouldn't cut it with Kevy. On their first meeting, he'd get down on his knees, hold her hand, say what he wanted, and slip the ring onto her finger. Maybe he'd even remove the old ring she'd been wearing since their wedding and replace it with the new one.

Zoe took him to the gold *souk*—the well-known gold market dominated by people of South Asian origin who did a brisk business there. Nigel selected the ring and let Zoe handle the negotiations. Zoe was in her element as she haggled effectively with the salespeople, clearly enjoying the bargaining process, which went on for quite a while as Nigel waited patiently.

He was not fully convinced as to how effective the haggling was in reducing the price, but he had to admit it was fun. He enjoyed the coffee—the Arabic kava in small cups. He figured it was all a part of the system developed over time to cater to each purchaser's expectations. He enjoyed the bargaining process but preferred what he was used to instead—buying at the sticker price—as it was simple, straightforward, and elegant.

At their apartment, Nigel spent most of the day packing and relaxing. He had a quiet dinner by himself in the kitchen, since both Jim and Zoe had to go out.

After a restful night, Zoe and Jim accompanied him to the Dubai airport early that morning. Nigel looked at them and said, "You know, I'll never forget all you did for me and Kevy. I'm not sure I'd have succeeded without you, so thanks a lot. You guys are true friends. I'll keep you informed. On our way back, we may stop over here for a few days on our way back to Toronto.

"Zoe, darling, you've helped me so much in handling the situation and planning out my path to reconciliation with Kevy and I'll never forget all the tips I got from both of you."

Tears welled up in Zoe's eyes. He patted her shoulder, gave Jim a bear hug and warmly shook his hand, turned around, and walked to the departure gate. The ring in his hand looked beautiful in the aircraft. He read the certificate of authenticity the shopkeeper had given him and went over his lines again.

# 13

During her flight from Dubai to Bengaluru, Kevina settled into her seat, feeling happier than she'd felt in a long time. Though she'd lost her financially rewarding assignment in Iran, perhaps forever, and she'd soon have to start looking for another similar contract.

But that wasn't a current concern.

She felt happy and optimistic that the sudden jolt she'd given Nigel by walking out on him had woken him up from his decades-long, self-centred slumber. He now appeared to be a man trying to reinvent his relationship with her. She was prepared to bury the unpleasant and painful past forever. Though wouldn't be able to forget it, she'd certainly do all she could to forgive, begin anew, and move forward, and resolved to be as optimistic as possible. From now on, she'd look for the positives in him and help him where she could as they went forward in their life together.

Thinking about the past, Surin came to her mind. She remembered the night they'd shared and the delight she'd felt, but that was a chapter that had to be closed forever. She resolved to dismiss it from her mind and try her best never to think about it again.

Across the aisle from her, Dave was already likely planning for his next assignments. Later, she thought he might be dozing, finally having relaxed in the comfort of the aircraft.

He was a fascinating man with an unusual job. She'd come to respect the man, what he stood for, and the institution he worked for, even for his cutting sense of humor. People like him were the unheralded guardians of our civilization, though they were condemned to oblivion. She wanted to ask him some questions but knew this wasn't the time. She thought that, someday, she might take on the challenge of writing about him and her experience in Iran. But at that moment, her own life provided enough challenges to her.

As the aircraft touched down on the runway at Bengaluru, she saw Nigel's flight details and arrival time on her palmtop. She had less than twenty-four hours before she'd see him. Rather than go to the airport to receive him, she thought she'd send a limo, wait to greet him as he arrived at the hotel, and go from there.

Upon arrival at the terminal building, a young Indian man approached Dave. They glanced quickly at each other's passes, and then both Dave and Kevina were whisked through Indian customs and immigration formalities. A special, diplomatic visa was stamped on her passport by a polite and smiling young lady. Kevina was a bit on edge as they passed through customs because she'd heard about the bureaucracy bordering on harassment tourists were sometimes subjected to upon entering India. She wanted to ask Dave a few questions about the process, but she knew there was no point asking him anything because he simply wouldn't give a straight answer. Maybe it was best for both of them that way.

Once outside, the young man looked at Kevina with a smile and said, "Welcome to India, madam. I hope you have a very pleasant stay here."

"Thank you very much." She didn't know his name, but she smiled at him and added, "Sir."

The terminal building was spacious, well-planned, and very pleasant, indeed. The young man continued to talk to Dave in low tones as they walked out of the airport and went straight to a waiting limo. When Dave and Kevina got into the backseat of the limo and the young man closed the door behind them, waved, and walked away. Kevina overcame the temptation to quiz Dave on the man as the limo sped away from the airport.

Dave said, "That was our operative here, Kevy. Good man. We should be at the Maharaja in a half hour or so. At this hour, the traffic should be a bit lighter, but during rush hours, it could take well over an hour to do the same trip."

This was Kevina's first visit to India.

She looked out and saw the narrow roads, already full of traffic of all descriptions: cars, trucks, tractors, rickshaws, bikes, people on foot, and animals. For her, there was an excitement in the air at what would occur in a land so different from what she'd been used to. She looked at the world unfolding before her with positivity and hope.

Dave said, "You know, I've been here many, many times over the past several decades. One is generally safe in most parts of India, people are friendly, though the salespeople are quite pushy."

He laughed and continued, "Over the past few decades, India has changed for the better. The changes, mostly addressing fundamental issues initiated by one of India's most popular and successful prime ministers, have been and continue to be implemented. India is much cleaner, organized, and safer than ever before.

"You'll be safe at the hotel, of course. Play the tourist with your hubby, see the sights, go on tours organized by the hotel—if there are any problems, please call me immediately. Don't get concerned if you don't see much of me, as I'm going to be quite busy here, but I'll keep in touch with you and let you know when you can head back home to Canada. As usual, we'll communicate in secure mode, only." He pointed at her palmtop in her hand.

"How can I ever thank you for what you've done, actually saving our lives? Could my husband, Surin, and I at least take you out for dinner as a token of our gratitude for all your help?"

"Sure, Kevy. I'd be delighted to have dinner with you. I'll certainly let you know when over the next few days, okay?" He laughed.

He seemed greatly appreciative of her offer. She'd purposely included Surin in her invitation and wondered whether he was aware of her dalliance with Surin. Men like him were paid to keep their mouths shut, do their duty, and move on. This was just as well because she wanted to close the issue finally and firmly. She continued looking out at the streets at the shops that were just opening and ready for business. The traffic increased, and the dust thickened.

The Maharaja was luxuriously decorated, which was a bit at odds with the street scene outside, but she and Dave were greeted with smiles, welcomes, and glasses of champagne, which Kevina declined but Dave didn't.

"Dr. Paul, you're all set," Dave said after they'd checked in. "Take care. We'll be in touch, for sure." Dave extended his hand.

Was this their final goodbye? Would she really see him again? She wanted to give him a goodbye kiss on his cheek. Instead, she accepted the extended hand. Dave turned and hurried toward the elevator. She asked the receptionist to arrange for a pickup at the airport for Nigel, but she was told it was all in hand, and led by the porter to her room.

She did about thirty minutes of yoga and meditation in her room, took a quick shower, and walked down the stairs to the lobby. It was a very large, impressive lobby, with clusters of luxurious sofas set around a snack bar, open around the clock. She decided to sit on one of the sofas the next day, in view of the main entrance and the reception desk, which would be the perfect spot to meet Nigel. She planned to arrive a few minutes before ten in the morning, sip some tea, and wait for his arrival.

She set off to explore the hotel. She wouldn't go out that day, but she'd find out all she could about the very large and opulent hotel. She'd also look at tour options and remain on her feet as much as possible that day so she'd sleep well in the night and be fresh for Nigel's arrival in about eighteen hours.

The next morning she got up early, checked her palmtop, and confirmed Nigel's flight was right on time. After a shower, she descended into the lobby and walked to the spot she'd selected; there was no one there. She settled down and asked the attendant for a large teapot and a bowl of oatmeal and fruit.

She checked her palmtop again—the flight had landed on schedule. There was a TV set with the morning news on, and while volume was low, she was able to see and follow the captions on the screen, though she'd have to move a bit closer to hear the commentator. None of that mattered as Kevy had other events on her mind.

She looked toward the entrance and saw a few travellers walk in and head straight for the reception desk accompanied by a uniformed limo driver. Nigel was among them, in the lead. He looked tanned and thin, his gait had speed and purpose. She felt her excitement rise. The receptionist greeted Nigel and started a conversation with him. While they talked, Nigel turned around, saw Kevy, and promptly abandoned the receptionist to hurry toward her.

She wanted to laugh at the sight of him running toward her. She stood up and with a big smile, started walking toward him. He'd clearly lost quite a bit of weight, which seemed to have renewed his aura and vigor. They met and fell into each other's arms, lingering in a hug.

Nigel slowly went down to his knees, opened a small jewelry box, and pulled out a ring. He held her hand in his, slowly removed the ring she had on, and slipped on the new one. By then, several people in the lobby, guests, and hotel employees alike, were watching them with delight.

"Kevy, darling, I am so, so sorry for having been such an insensitive oaf all this time. I've now realized the error of my ways and the totally inappropriate attitude I've had toward you. There's no one in my life who I love more, care more for, or is more precious than you. I've decided to change everything about me to win your love. Will you please give me another chance and accept me in your life as your husband forever? Let's make a new beginning and bring nothing but joy and happiness to each other's life."

Tears flowed down Kevina's face as she looked at Nigel to see genuine sincerity. She had a moment to collect her thoughts when the limo driver came to bid Nigel goodbye and collect his tip. Nigel quickly handed over a few Dubai dirhams to the driver, who accepted them with outpourings of gratitude, and then quickly left them.

"Yes, my dear Nigel, I love you, too, and yes, yes, and yes to all you have said. The ring is absolutely lovely." She kissed him.

He picked up his bag, and they walked to the elevator, arm in arm.

In the room, they settled on the couch. Nigel reached over and took Kevina's hand.

"Kevy, darling, I want to hear all about what happened in the country you were in when you are ready. On second thought, would you like to go to the bar with me, have a celebratory glass of wine, and talk about your recent activities and successes? What do you think?"

At the bar, they settled down in a corner, far away from the TV screens. Nigel chose a red wine, and when the waiter had poured it into their glasses, Nigel raised his glass to her.

"Kevy, I want you to know that I understand what you went through. I want to do all I can to make our lives together a most wonderful experience from this point on. Also, I want to thank you from the depth of my heart for this opportunity. Rest assured, Kevy, I'll do all I can to fill your life with happiness."

Kevina reached over and put her finger on his lips.

"I believe you completely, my darling. Here's to the rest of our lives together." She raised her wine glass to his and had a sip.

They put their glasses down and she kissed him. It wasn't a passionate kiss, but there was a deep sweetness to it. Deep in her heart, Kevina was filled with contentment. She looked into his eyes as her arms slid away from him and she raised her glass to him.

"Thanks, Nigel. You're already helping me. I want to say how sorry I am to have done what I did to you, but now that you're here, we can go forward together. I have a long story to tell you."

Kevina began to narrate the sequence of events from the day she walked out on him on their train journey, while Nigel listened attentively.

When she got into her activities in Iran, he realized that almost since the beginning of the twenty-first century, the world had entered into a state of perpetual war—a never-ending world war, the war between the ever-advancing human civilization and the dark forces that wanted to—and did, at times, with momentary successes—drag humanity back into the stone ages. In recent decades, the positive forces of civilization had performed wonders in the field of human health, the eradication of poverty, and scientific advancements, especially where robotics and aerospace were concerned. Humankind was on the precipice of major discoveries and advancement in space exploration. Regular travel to other planets in our solar system was not only distinctly possible but highly probable. Then there was this relatively small but surprisingly strong force of evil that continued to cause death and destruction almost anywhere. Nothing seemed beyond their reach. And now they had touched Kevina...almost.

Back in the room, they crawled into bed, and though they were both tired, they couldn't sleep. Kevina finished telling him everything that had happened since their train ride—well, almost everything. Nigel was attentive and understood her story.

"Kevy, darling, I'm amazed at your achievement, and truly, you may have saved a significant portion of the world from the hands of evil. I'm immensely proud of you. I know we can't mention any of this to anyone, but *I* know. You are, indeed, a giant, Kevy, and I'm glad to have this incredible opportunity to be your husband. Thank you for letting me back into your life. I want to tell you all about what I did in the last few weeks, too, but let's talk about it tomorrow, over breakfast."

With that, he got up to turn off the lights in their hotel bedroom. No sooner had he taken Kevina into his embrace, than she was deep in sleep. Compassion for each other was the need of the hour and the hours that followed. Passion had to take a backseat, at least for the time being. Locked in their embrace, they both fell into a deep sleep.

The next morning, he got up quite early. She was still deep in sleep, and he didn't want to wake her. He phoned room service and ordered two full breakfasts in an hour, hoping Kevina would be up by then, and dashed off to take a shower.

Just as he was about to turn off the shower faucet, he heard the shower door open, turned around, and saw Kevina stepping into the shower. She slid into his arms.

He realized, then, how beautiful she truly was. "Right here, in the shower?" he asked.

"Well, no, why don't you dry off, get into the bed, wait for me, and I'll see you in about three minutes."

A few minutes later, she sidled up to him in the bed, fresh and beautiful. Their lips met, and their arms wrapped around each other. Both began to breathe deeply, holding their breath and exhaling together as they explored each other.

Twenty minutes later, there was a knock on the door. "Room service."

"Kevy, stay in bed. I'll get the door."

Nigel arose, put his robe on, and opened the door. The attendant entered the room with a large tray, laid out the breakfast on the dining table, and left a copy of the *India Times* newspaper for them. Nigel signed the bill and the door closed behind the attendant.

"That was wonderful, Nigel, darling," Kevy said. She kissed him on his cheek and sat down at the table.

She hadn't felt this relaxed and content for a long time.

# 14

O ver the next few days, Kevina, Nigel, and Surin toured the area near Bengaluru. Surin had a few days of rest and recovery from his office, and he had decided to spend those days with Kevina and Nigel. Kevina appreciated Surin's presence, as he was able to efficiently guide them to all the tourist attractions. Nigel had mentioned to Kevina that Jim and Zoe in Dubai had highly recommended the ancient caves at Ajanta, and Surin readily agreed.

"Why don't we go there early tomorrow morning? The flight from Bengaluru is only an hour and a half to Aurangabad, near the caves. From the airport, we can go straight to the caves. It shouldn't be more than another hour and a half drive," Surin suggested.

Both Kevina and Nigel agreed.

Early the next morning, the three of them went by Air Bengaluru from Bengaluru, northward to Aurangabad, about a thousand kilometers. The flight was routine, and Kevina spent most of the time reviewing the literature on the caves and then dozing to catch up on some sleep. Nigel seemed to be engaged in a conversation, with Surin, providing background on India and the caves to Nigel.

The ride from the Aurangabad airport to the caves was very comfortable in a large taxi, driven by a charming, uniformed driver. In the backseat, Kevina and Nigel held hands and busied themselves looking out to the countryside as it unfolded on either side of the road. The one-hundred-kilometre road had been recently constructed, and the drive was smooth.

Over the past few decades, India seemed to have made considerable progress in upgrading its transportation infrastructure. In particular, India had made long-overdue, massive investments in upgrading the country's network of highway and roadways. As well, the government had invested in providing water and electricity for the more remote villages. The benefits of this development in India's infrastructure were clearly visible. The greatest positive and visible impact was in poverty reduction. Kevina knew that it was in the streets of a country where the real progress could be measured by simple observation. The look of the people, the manner in which they carried themselves, and the plight of towns and villages, told a positive story.

She couldn't help but feel good about India in general, even though she thought it still had some distance to go when compared to other Asian giants like China.

Kevina really enjoyed walking around the caves. Surin and Nigel walked together, while Kevina wanted to experience the caves on her own. She told Nigel to page her on her palmtop when they were done. She thought she might be able to awaken her DNA and see if her genes could find a link to the ancient civilization depicted in the statues and the paintings in the caves. She hired a young, official guide, recommended by the entrance ticket office. He said his name was Gautam.

It was very appropriate, Kevina thought, because the caves were a monument dedicated to Buddhism founded by Gautama Buddha, around 450 BCE. Kevina resisted the urge to question him on his name, whether it was truly so, or something contrived to impress the tourists.

Kevina remembered what she'd read about the advent of Buddhism and its tenets, some time ago. Gautam was, indeed, very knowledgeable, and spoke English well. He delivered his well-practiced lecture while they walked together.

The thirty or so Buddhist caves had been excavated and sculpted circa 200 BCE. About eight hundred years later, the caves were inexplicably abandoned and then forgotten. The arrival of Islam in India around AD 800 sounded the death knell for Buddhism, which disappeared almost totally from the land of its birth.

By then, Buddhism had not only spread to the Far East and Southeast Asia but had also continued to evolve. Interestingly, such countries as Thailand, China, and Japan, which had adopted the more flexible version of the religion, like Mahayana, seemed to maintain their independence against foreign invasions and progress ahead.

It wasn't until the early nineteenth century that John Smith—who was with a tiger-hunting party—rediscovered the Ajanta Caves, which had remained hidden for almost a thousand years. The British government of India had them excavated to reveal the splendor of the ancient civilization during the Maurya-Gupta dynasty, about two thousand years ago, to the world.

What impressed Kevina even more, was the philosophy of Mahayana Buddhism, which expected all humans to be self-reliant, not ask for assistance from God, and believe that all of its followers could rise up intellectually to attain enlightenment. Kindness to all, non-violence, compassion, and tolerance were the key pillars of Mahayana.

The guide had already begun wrapping up his tour when she heard him say, "The Buddha, on his deathbed, said to his followers, 'After my death, do not rely on others for help. Be a lamp to yourself, and he who relies on himself only and not on others and holds fast to the truth shall attain the very highest summit.'"

Over the next few weeks, she thought a lot about lighting the lamp within her and doing what she could to attain greatness. She'd always been interested in extending her lifespan, and with it, good health. She knew the path to attaining healthy longevity involved not only being physically sound, but also cultivating and improving mental faculties, and seeking within her a higher level of morality.

She already had a reputation for being a fitness nut. Now she would extend her nuttiness beyond the physical realm.

She heard a female voice say, "Lost her again. Her BP's falling rapidly. Her peripheral systems have begun to shut down. Must stop the bleeding."

The voice faded away to a mere whisper. She felt intense pain and warm blood flowing from her lower abdomen while the rest of her body felt very cold. She thought about the pain and that she'd never experienced such pain before. She whimpered, inhaled deeply, held her breath, and slowly exhaled. The pain continued. She thought she heard Nigel's voice from far away.

She opened her eyes. She was in a hospital bed, surrounded by people in white coats. She tried to get up, but the woman next to her put a gentle hand on her shoulder, motioned for her to remain still, and said, "Dr. Paul, you are in a hospital. Remember the aircraft you were piloting crashed? Your injury wasn't very serious, but during the delay in your rescue, you lost a lot of blood. Now you have sizable, intra-abdominal hematoma. The doctors here have worked around the clock to stop the bleeding, transfuse blood, and treat your condition. Can you hear me?"

She began to slide back into semi-consciousness and found it difficult to focus her attention to the doctor, but deep down, she remembered.

After her arrival in India, now reunited with Nigel, she enjoyed the bliss of her newly rekindled love with him. Nigel had just retired, and upon her recommendation, he enrolled in an international MBA program, offered through the department of distance learning at the Canadian e-University. She'd decided to take what she thought was a well-deserved break. She read, went for long walks—mostly with Nigel—and played tennis—also with Nigel.

The deeply rooted lure of aviation continued to beckon to her. She had to do some flying to renew her pilot's license, and she'd recently checked out on the latest Saturn aircraft. The Saturn was an all-composite aircraft, with an electronic cockpit, and a hybrid engine that was essentially electric, but with a clean-burning biofuel engine as a backup. The latest innovations in engine-battery technology had made the Saturn the greenest aircraft of its type, with a virtually zero, carbon footprint.

She was at Bengaluru International Airport's general aviation area and completed her pre-flight check on the aircraft. She fired up the engine and watched the electronic aircraft management system automatically configure the aircraft parameters for taxiing and takeoff upon reaching the takeoff point at the runway. The EAMS would subsequently, at the right times, configure the aircraft for cruising, descent, final approach, and landing. The aircraft could complete its entire itinerary automatically—with the pilot merely monitoring the functioning of the aircraft.

That day, her two-hour itinerary for pleasure flying in the Bengaluru area was programmed in the EAMS, which automatically communicated with the air traffic management system. She saw the air traffic instructions flash on her screen. Voice communications were only used to resolve unusual situations, like emergencies. It was impersonal, perhaps, but it was effective, efficient, and safe.

The Saturn reached cruising altitude at eight thousand feet. As the world unfolded below her, she enjoyed the stunning view from up above. Besides a euphoric, almost therapeutic feeling, flying also gave her time to contemplate. Once in the air, she always felt detached from her earthly reality, and at peace with herself. The cockpit of the aircraft at that very moment defined her world. Everything else seemed distant and at that very moment, almost irrelevant.

About an hour out, she noticed the engine had coughed, but the EAMS indicated "Ops norm". Minutes later, the engine stopped. She hit the engine-reset button on the EAMS, which was already sending the SOS messages to the ATC. The EAMS configured the aircraft for emergency descent while she visually searched for a safe spot for an emergency landing. She picked the nearest farm and manually took control of the aircraft from the EAMS for a landing without panic, her actions fluid, almost routine. The last thing she remembered was the strong smell of bio-avgas in the cockpit, the aircraft undershooting the landing spot into some trees, flipping over, and then a black void.

Kevina heard a voice, sounding like her own. "This is it, Kevy," it said. "This is the end of the line. You're dying and going to enter the world beyond. Now, you'll finally know if there really is a God. Now's the time to think about what you'll say to Him. More importantly, what He'll say to you as you appear before Him. Will He say, 'So, you've had doubts about Me and now here you are'?"

Kevina felt as if she were sinking into a deep chasm. There was darkness all around her. She continued to plunge into the abyss of blackness for a long time. She tried to look up, and far away, she saw a bright light source, looking every bit like a distant star. She continued to look at it, extended her hand, and tried to reach out.

She saw a lady in white emerge from the star, floating toward her. The lady extended her hand as she quickly closed in on Kevina. Now Kevina could see her face. The women smiled and said, "No, Kevy, don't listen to your other self.

Listen to me. Pull yourself out, use your incredible mental power to overcome your present state, step out of this moment, and look forward to full recovery and beyond. You can, must, and will do it. Help the doctors help you. You can will yourself to health and even longevity."

Do not go gentle into that good night...Rage, rage against the dying of the light

Kevy reached out to her, but the woman faded away, repeating the lines from the Dylan Thomas poem. She thought her face had resembled Shelly. Could it have been Shelly in adult form talking to her?

Then she heard the doctor. "Her BP's rising, now at ninety over sixty, heartbeat at eighty, and lowering. The bleeding's stopped. Let's go ahead with the Coumadin treatment."

This was the pivotal moment, the life-altering tipping point for Kevina. There was no magic potion, except harnessing the power of the mind with a positive, proactive attitude, regular physical and mental exercise, long meditative walks, and a healthy diet.

Kevy rapidly progressed to a full recovery.

Meanwhile, the Aviation Accident Investigation Authority convened an inquiry into the cause of Kevina's air crash, and she had to provide a statement as to the events leading up to the accident. Finally, the AAIA formally released their findings. The cause of the air crash was attributed to faulty software in the autopilot's flight management system. It was revealed that under certain circumstances, the FMS initiated an automatic shutdown of the engine. The investigation report commended Kevina's conduct as the pilot on record, and no blame was apportioned to her. There was, however, considerable debate in aviation circles and in the public media whether the dramatic increase in the reliance on automation was a serious problem, and whether it might worsen over time.

Identified software problems in that type of aircraft were immediately fixed and exhaustively tested by the aircraft manufacturer. Pilot training standards and practices were scrutinized and upgraded to allow training for various modes of failure. The progress in aviation technology continued its march ahead, as did Kevina's health.

Over the decades ahead, her unique algorithm for longevity, kept the forces of advancing age at bay, preserving her youthfulness well beyond her nineties. Upon becoming a centenarian, already a celebrity, frequently invited as guest speaker at various professional, social, and political events, she continued to educate the world about her elixir for longevity and good health.

She and Nigel lived together for several decades. They travelled together, the world over. One morning, Nigel didn't wake up; he passed away at age ninety-nine. Though deeply saddened, Kevina taught herself to accept the loss and move on. She and Nigel had discussed the matter of death several times, and both had promised the other they'd seek closure of the long chapter in life between them, and look ahead.

During Nigel's funeral, the coffin carrying his body was placed in the cremation chamber. The crematorium official looked at her and said, "Dr. Paul, please go ahead and press the button."

She took a deep breath, unsure of what she should think, murmured to herself, "Goodbye, Nigel. I love you," and pressed the button. The large oven, which was already set at over a thousand degrees Celsius, commenced to consuming the body. She lingered for a few minutes, remembering Nigel's advice: "Kevy, my love, I know I'll go on that one-way journey alone, well before you. When that happens, look into yourself and draw from your very large reservoir of strength to move up in every way. I'd very much like for you to do that: to close our chapter together and move on."

She continued her involvement in public speaking, taking a minimum fee for herself and asking the sponsors to contribute the rest to various national and international charities. She soon found herself on several boards of charitable foundations.

# 15

At the age of 137, Kevy was finally, no more. She now belonged to the realm of history and memories.

The quest for longevity is an unfulfilled desire of humanity. Medical technology can add a few years to the winter of life with some success, but by simply extending old age without necessarily renewing youthfulness. However, Kevy, along with adding decades to her lifespan, had found a fountain of health and vitality. Was she simply an inexplicable freak of nature, or had she truly unlocked that secret of longevity that is perhaps buried deep within all humans? Can one truly will oneself to good health? Discovering the powers of mind will continue to remain a challenge for future generations to address.

I felt that my magazine assignment was supposed to focus on her full life and her greatest achievement—that of longevity and good health.

The funeral was an unusual event as no tears were shed. It was a beautiful Sunday afternoon. The well-manicured cemetery, just north of Toronto, was bathed in golden sunshine, under a bright blue and clear sky. There was also a sublime sadness to the air, but maybe that was just my state of mind. The afternoon wore on as several local politicians made short speeches, touching on the philanthropic aspects of Kevina's life. The references to other aspects of her life remained shrouded in superficiality. I knew the most about her life but hadn't been asked to speak, which was fine with me, as I felt I couldn't possibly do justice to her in a few words. I'd already written her life's story, besides.

All in attendance spoke about how they'd miss her, but I'd miss her on a much deeper level. In writing about her, I'd touched her soul, her innermost feelings and thoughts, and her loves in life. She'd been in love with several people at different times in her life.

There was a call for three minutes of silence in her memory, in which we all participated, and for a long time afterward, her presence lingered over us. We all felt it, and I felt it in particular.

During her funeral, the editor in chief of my magazine had told me to see him the next day in the office, and I did.

"There you are. I thought the mayor did a good job yesterday at the funeral, calling it a celebration of Kevina's life."

I nodded, and he continued, "In view of her passing, I think we should go to publication with what you have so far. We can do the second part later. The national and global media have noted her demise. Social media's abuzz with people acknowledging her death and commenting on her long life, so our timing would be very appropriate, and I am going to publication with what you have so far, ASAP—like early next week."

I saw his unchallengeable rationale and simply nodded.

I left his office a bit saddened as I remembered her words: "When in a saddened mood, go for a walk in the woods. Look for comfort in nature." I put on my jacket and walked over to the crematorium where we'd been the day before, and walked around the beautiful cemetery grounds. I went over to her plaque, laid the previous day, dedicated to her memory. There was a pile of flowers around the plaque, but I hadn't brought any flowers to place.

The clouds darkened and it began to drizzle. I stood there, in the rain, to say my final goodbye to her, and walked back to my office.

Goodbye, Kevina. Until we later meet.

Manufactured by Amazon.ca
Bolton, ON